YOU SHOULD BE
SO LUC

S0-BYF-105

A New Comedy

by Charles Busch

SAMUEL FRENCH, INC.
45 WEST 25TH STREET   NEW YORK 10010
7623 SUNSET BOULEVARD HOLLYWOOD 90046
LONDON   TORONTO

3

IMPORTANT BILLING AND CREDIT REQUIREMENTS

You Should Be So Lucky opened in New York City on November 2, 1994. It was produced by Primary Stages, Casey Childs, Artistic Director in association with The Herrick Theatre Foundation. It was directed by Kenneth Elliott. The Production Stage Manager was John Frederick Sullivan. The cast (in order of appearance) was as follows:

MR. ROSENBERG --------------Stephen Pearlman

CHRISTOPHER ---------------------Charles Busch

POLLY---------------------------------- Nell Campbell

WALTER----------------------------- Matthew Arkin

LENORE ------------------------------ Julie Halston

WANDA WANG----------------------- Jennifer Kato

TIME & PLACE

The Present.

A small railroad apartment in Greenwich Village. We are in the living room. A door up left leads outside and an archway up right, covered with a curtain of beads, leads off to a kitchen and bedroom. The decor is a mad combination of Chinese kitsch and Art Nouveau, all collected for next to nothing at flea markets. The walls are crowded with antique fans and samurai swords. The dominating feature of the room is a large Victorian sofa, smothered in heavily fringed velvet throws and pillows. Once one becomes accustomed to the fake opulence of the room, one notices the cracked moldy walls and half-stripped woodwork.

It's mid-afternoon, on a hot summer day.

YOU SHOULD BE SO LUCKY

ACT I

Scene 1

MR. ROSENBERG enters from the archway with an old-fashioned ice pack. HE is a tall, imposing man in his sixties, dressed in a beautifully tailored suit. HE projects an elegant elder statesman quality and also a cuddly grandfatherly warmth. His speech still retains a trace of his Lower East Side roots.

ROSENBERG. (*Talking to someone in the kitchen.*) This is really quite a place, (*Up center, to himself.*) quite a place. So many things. (*To himself.*) What does it remind me of? A whorehouse in Shanghai or my Aunt Basha's apartment in Riverdale? (*To the person in the kitchen.*) Please accept this in the spirit in which it's intended, Christopher, I realize I'm a complete stranger, but you really should find yourself a good plasterer. These walls ... (*Muttering to himself.*) *ah zoy tzebrachn mir kin platzn.* (*To the person in the kitchen.*) You should have your landlord replace these old windows. You'd be amazed at how much heat you'll save in the winter. Keep in mind these are just suggestions.

(CHRISTOPHER enters from the kitchen holding a tray of tea things. HE is a very boyish young man in his early thirties. HE is an eccentric blend of intense timidity and equally intense enthusiasm.)

CHRISTOPHER. Here's your tea, Mr. Rosenberg. What are you doing standing up?

ROSENBERG. I'm fine. I'm perfectly fine.

CHRISTOPHER. You fainted on the sidewalk. Thank you very much. *(Sets tea on the coffee table.)*

ROSENBERG. I am feeling much better. *(Switching subjects quickly.)* Christopher, this could be a charming apartment. High ceilings.

CHRISTOPHER. I really should fix it up, I suppose. But you know, I'm the kind of person who never likes being tied down to any one place. I never know how long I'm going to stay.

ROSENBERG. How long have you been here?

CHRISTOPHER. Twelve years. Sugar?

ROSENBERG. Please.

CHRISTOPHER. It's been quite a while since I've entertained anyone.

ROSENBERG. How long's it been?

CHRISTOPHER. Twelve years. Milk?

ROSENBERG. No. Thank you.

CHRISTOPHER. *(Handing him a teacup.)* Here you go. Here's your tea.

ROSENBERG. This is a fine piece of china. You really should get that chip repaired.

CHRISTOPHER. I really should. It hasn't been broken very long.

ROSENBERG. How long?

CHRISTOPHER. Twelve years. Are you sure you should be moving around?

ROSENBERG. It was just a little dizziness.

CHRISTOPHER. No, you blacked out completely.

ROSENBERG. This humidity is deadly for senior citizens.

CHRISTOPHER. Maybe you should see a doctor. I'm very close to St. Vincent's.

ROSENBERG. I'm fine. I'm just lucky that I didn't hit my head on the pavement. Christopher, you're a true Samaritan; bringing me into your apartment, a complete and total stranger. Please, let me give you something for your generosity. (*HE puts his teacup down on the coffee table and takes out his wallet.*)

CHRISTOPHER. Please, put that away.

ROSENBERG. (*Handing him money.*) There's a marvelous seafood restaurant on Hudson Street. Have a Surf and Turf on me.

CHRISTOPHER. You'll hurt my feelings if you go on like that.

ROSENBERG. You're quite a kid. (*Putting the money away and slowly crossing up right and then to up center.*)

CHRISTOPHER. My mother was a nurse. I guess I take after her.

ROSENBERG. (*Seeing a framed photo on the table.*) Are these your parents?

CHRISTOPHER. Yes.

ROSENBERG. A handsome couple.

CHRISTOPHER. That was their wedding photo.

ROSENBERG. Are they still living?

CHRISTOPHER. (*Crossing right and up to him.*) No, they both died when I was very young. They were both extraordinary people. My mother was not only a nurse but a poet, a flautist and a champion figure skater.

ROSENBERG. Oh my.

CHRISTOPHER. (*Picking up and displaying a tray from furthest up table.*) These are her medals. And my father was a horseman, a puppeteer and a piano tuner. (*Picking up an object from the sofa table just above sofa.*) This was his pitch pipe.

ROSENBERG. Are you musical?

CHRISTOPHER. Oh no. I'm afraid I didn't inherit much from them. Even the clutter I found for myself.

ROSENBERG. (*Crossing down right around barber chair to right of it.*) This is a nice old-fashioned piece of furniture. Are you a barber?

CHRISTOPHER. (*Crossing down to left of barber chair opposite Rosenberg.*) I'm an electrologist. (*ROSENBERG looks puzzled.*) An electrologist. I remove unwanted hair from people.

ROSENBERG. Really? You went to school for this?

CHRISTOPHER. Oh yes. I'm a trained professional.

ROSENBERG. Is it painful, this … plucking?

CHRISTOPHER. More discomfort than pain. And we do not pluck. We do not pluck. I just get livid when ignorant people dismiss us as mere pluckers. (*Showing him a chart, just above barber chair.*) I have a needle with an electric charge that destroys the papilla, the seed of the hair directly below the root. I can show you before and after photos of my clients. You probably wouldn't be interested.

ROSENBERG. No, I would. Please. (*CHRISTOPHER hesitates.*) No, I really would. Show me.

CHRISTOPHER. Okay. (*CHRISTOPHER crosses tentatively left to desk.*)

ROSENBERG. I admire a fellow who's enthusiastic about his work.

CHRISTOPHER. (*Putting down teacup, HE opens top drawer of desk and rifles through a bunch of papers.*) I can almost be obsessive. My sister, Polly, says I'm a natural born electrologist because I have a great need to smooth things over. Here they are. (*Takes out an envelope with photos and crosses down left to better light by window, urging Rosenberg to join him.*) This is Miss Fernandez. She's from New Rochelle. Here she is before.

ROSENBERG. (*Crossing to Christopher's right.*) Oh my, the poor woman. We used to call those mutton chop whiskers.

CHRISTOPHER. It was a challenge. Even then I thought she was a handsome woman. When she wore black, she looked rather like Johnny Cash. (*Finding another photo.*) Here she is several months later. Isn't she gorgeous?

ROSENBERG. Sort of a prettier Anthony Quinn.

CHRISTOPHER. (*Abruptly putting photos back in envelope.*) I'm sorry if I fail to find that amusing. We worked very hard for nearly a year clearing up her ... um, whiskers.

ROSENBERG. Forgive me for being flip.

CHRISTOPHER. If you could have seen her expression of pure joy when we finally got rid of her moustache. Her face is my greatest achievement, my *Schindler's List*.

ROSENBERG. You're very deep.

CHRISTOPHER. Not really. It's just that my superficiality is rather complex. (*HE crosses up and returns photos to desk drawer.*)

ROSENBERG. You know, Christopher, I might be in the market for your services. It's this little bit on my back and shoulders. A light dusting that could use some electrolysizing. Do you think that's terribly vain or womanish of me?

CHRISTOPHER. Au contraire, Mr. Rosenberg. I applaud your vanity. Bravo. (*Striking an unconsciously effeminate pose.*) There is nothing effeminate about good grooming.

ROSENBERG. I'm thinking about making a few changes in my life. My wife died just over two years ago. She was a remarkable woman. We had a forty-two year romance. Are you married?

CHRISTOPHER. No.

ROSENBERG. Y'ever been married? Engaged?

CHRISTOPHER. No. I'm afraid I'm the cat that walks alone.

ROSENBERG. My friend, you're missing out on something.

CHRISTOPHER. I am passionate about my work *and* my hobbies. (*Pointing to shelf above desk.*) I paint goblin faces on dried yams.

ROSENBERG. Yams? Well, um, recently I told myself, "Enough already, stop with the grieving, get on with your life." Perhaps I'm a fool but I thought I'd try dating again. (*Crossing to center of sofa.*) Perhaps I should make a few improvements to give myself a more attractive appearance. (*Sitting.*) How much do you charge?

CHRISTOPHER. Forty dollars for an hour's session. That's pretty standard. You can check if you want but I don't bargain. I'm a trained professional. (*Insecure.*) You think that's too much?

ROSENBERG. No, no. I thought it would be more. I have no plans for the rest of the afternoon. Could we start right now? Unless you have other appointments.

CHRISTOPHER. (*Crossing up to desk and retrieving his appointment book.*) I may. Let me see. Hmmm. (*It's empty.*) I think I can fit you in.

(*There's loud POUNDING on the front door.*)

POLLY. (*Outside.*) Christopher! Open up! I need you! I know you're in there!

CHRISTOPHER. My sister Polly.

ROSENBERG. (*Getting up.*) You'd better answer it. We'll do this some other time.

CHRISTOPHER. No, you'll never come back. And it's been so slow.

POLLY. (*Outside.*) Please let me in!

ROSENBERG. She sounds like she's in trouble.

CHRISTOPHER. She's an unemployed actress. Her entire union's in trouble.

POLLY. (*Outside.*) Christopher, please!

(*CHRISTOPHER crosses left and up, opens the door and POLLY falls in. A flamboyant, jazzy redhead. SHE lugs in some suitcases, shopping bags, a hat box and a dead looking plant. SHE immediately drops everything, save the plant, which SHE deposits on the desk. SHE speaks in a lovely British accent.*)

POLLY. Thank God!

CHRISTOPHER. What is all this?

POLLY. The effects of a lifetime. (*Seeing Rosenberg.*) Please sir, whoever you are, move a little to the right. (*Crossing down to left of sofa.*) I need to fling myself on that divan. I can't even fling. I'm quite beyond the dramatic gesture. (*In a fit of tears, SHE throws herself dramatically onto the sofa.*)

CHRISTOPHER. (*Crossing down to left of sofa.*) Polly, this is Mr. Rosenberg.

POLLY. (*Not yet recovered.*) Yes.

CHRISTOPHER. What happened?

POLLY. (*Sitting up.*) Sam threw me out. Out into the streets.

CHRISTOPHER. Polly, you must get your name on a lease. You can't go on like this.

POLLY. What do you mean? Never before has a man tossed my clothes out of an eighth floor window. No, I should never have involved myself with someone so much younger.

CHRISTOPHER. And so volatile.

POLLY. You don't know how many nights I feared for my life. He can't accept that he's a failure. A failed playwright.

CHRISTOPHER. He's only twenty-four.

POLLY. He failed before he began!

CHRISTOPHER. I hadn't heard from you in a month.

POLLY. Darling, I was his prisoner in the San Remo. I might as well have been in Kuwait. The whole situation came to a boil when I flung his damned manuscript into the fire and watched it burn.

ROSENBERG. (*Sitting sofa right, next to her.*) You destroyed his play? I can see why he was miffed.

CHRISTOPHER. I hope it was only a one act.

POLLY. It was a verse trilogy. The play was his child and I gladly watched it turn to ashes. Burn! Burn! I'm burning your child!

CHRISTOPHER. Polly played Hedda Gabler in Tulsa. I saw it. She was absolutely brilliant.

POLLY. My greatest fan.

ROSENBERG. Polly, you sound British.

POLLY. Well, I've lived for many years in England.

CHRISTOPHER. She studied at The Royal Academy and played one season in Manchester.

POLLY. Two seasons.

ROSENBERG. (*To Christopher.*) Pardon me for saying this, but, you talk a little funny too.

CHRISTOPHER. I spent a long weekend with her.

ROSENBERG. Where are you both from originally?

CHRISTOPHER/POLLY. Albuquerque.

CHRISTOPHER. Polly, what are you going to do?

POLLY. Start again. Somewhere. Somehow. Frankly, I'm at your mercy.

CHRISTOPHER. It's a very small apartment.

POLLY. But I can make myself useful. I can do manicures and pedicures. It'll be better than me paying you rent. (*To Rosenberg.*) Darling, let me see those cuticles.

CHRISTOPHER. Leave him alone. (*Crossing up left and picking up her luggage.*) What can I say? I guess you've already moved in. Is this it?

POLLY. My entire world.

CHRISTOPHER. (*Noticing the plant on the desk.*) Why'd you save that dead plant?

POLLY. That plant is far from dead. That plant is nesting.

CHRISTOPHER. It's an amaryllis?!

POLLY. The most glorious amaryllis. And it's due to bloom some time early fall. We have to set it in the bottom of a closet in the dark. I promise you, Christopher, I will have my own place before it blooms. (*CHRISTOPHER crosses right, exiting with her luggage into the archway up right.*) Mr. Rosenberg, what line of work are you in?

ROSENBERG. I'm in the financial world. I advise.

POLLY. (*Flirtatiously.*) How I wish I had some assets you could advise me on.

CHRISTOPHER. Stop flirting with him. Don't take her seriously. She's always acting.

ROSENBERG. Frankly, I was enjoying the performance.

POLLY. (*Rising and taking a deep curtsy.*) Thank you.

CHRISTOPHER. (*Crossing left, down around coffee table and Polly to desk. HE picks up his cup of tea.*) Polly gets everything she wants simply through charm. I've been her slave all my life.

ROSENBERG. I can see why. She's a very vivacious young lady.

CHRISTOPHER. And totally selfish and egocentric.

POLLY. I've had to make my own way in the world. I've had a less than spectacular career in the theatre and it's left scars.

CHRISTOPHER. Oh, you were this way when you used to drown my dolls in the bathtub.

POLLY. I didn't.

CHRISTOPHER. Have you forgotten "Titantic Barbie"?

POLLY. Well, I always resuscitated her. Now, I need to do the same for you.

CHRISTOPHER. Here we go.

POLLY. It's kismet that brought me here. You need me. You live like some pathetic eccentric immersed in a world of shadows and dusty corners. Meet my brother, Miss Havisham.

CHRISTOPHER. You really have a lot of nerve barging in here and asking for my help and then criticizing me. I have a very full life. I provide a service that frees people from society's unjust stigma against excessive body hair. I have a wonderful family of loyal friends.

POLLY. Oh cool down. You're so touchy about the slightest bit of criticism. (*Crossing in to Rosenberg at sofa.*) Mr. Rosenberg, my brother and I are both classic examples of adult children of alcoholics.

CHRISTOPHER. Who was an alcoholic?

POLLY. Mother was. Believe me, Chris, I know a lot about this. Adult children of alcoholics find it impossible to complete things. I've never seen you finish a crossword puzzle or a plate of escargot. Classic.

CHRISTOPHER. But Mother wasn't an alcoholic.

POLLY. How would you know? You were only nine when she fell out the window. I was eleven and keenly perceptive.

CHRISTOPHER. But Polly …

POLLY. (*Getting up.*) Mother was a drunk! Don't argue with me! And you're going to follow in her wobbling footsteps. An alcoholic drinks out of loneliness and frustration.

CHRISTOPHER. Are you finished?

POLLY. I'm just getting revved up.

CHRISTOPHER. Mr. Rosenberg, I'm really sorry. This strange woman has some fixation that I'm her brother. Why don't you go into the bedroom and change. There's a kimono on a hook inside the armoire.

ROSENBERG. (*Repeating.*) In the armoire. (*HE exits.*)

CHRISTOPHER. (*Crossing right to sofa center, picking up tea tray.*) Polly, you really are wrong. I'm not lonely. I do have friends. Close friends. Norma Leeds, for one. (*Crossing right, up and around sofa, depositing tea tray on sofa table up center.*)

POLLY. (*Crossing left to window seat.*) She's ninety-two and hasn't spoken since her last stroke.

CHRISTOPHER. Um … Steven Deautsch.

POLLY. He's ten years old. Who do you think you are? Michael Jackson? (*Sitting on window seat.*)

CHRISTOPHER. (*Crossing down right, around to right of barber chair. HE removes a decorative lamp shade from the gooseneck surgical lamp above chair.*) Roger Bernstein's my age.

POLLY. I'm surprised you don't count him as three people.

CHRISTOPHER. He's on a different medication now. (*Putting lamp shade on stool, just below archway up right.*)

POLLY. (*Getting back up.*) These aren't friends. These are cases.

CHRISTOPHER. (*Impatiently. Opening electrolysis cabinet on wall behind chair.*) Polly, I have work to do.

POLLY. (*Quickly crossing up to above desk, indicating plant on desk.*) Christopher, look at that plant. You are that amaryllis.

CHRISTOPHER. (*Wearily. Turning barber chair to face upstage and adjusting seat back into a prone position.*) Oh Polly …

POLLY. You are that amaryllis. You've been in decades of withdrawal, alone in a dark closet.

CHRISTOPHER. This symbolism is really hokey. (*HE turns on the electrolysis machine. We hear a HUM.*)

POLLY. I'm an actress, not a playwright.

CHRISTOPHER. (*HE grabs a length of paper towel from underneath cabinet and places it over the barber chair.*) I was doing so fine ...

POLLY. No you weren't. Christopher, you have no life. You have excuses to be busy.

CHRISTOPHER. (*Pulling down surgical lamp, so that it is directly over chair.*) Enough already. (*Crossing left between sofa and coffee table, to Polly.*) You want me to admit that things are grim? Well alright, things are very grim. Mr. Rosenberg is the first client I've had in weeks. New York Magazine won't even take my ads anymore. I owe them too much money. Make your phone calls now, darling, because I don't know how much longer we'll have a telephone. My few friends, if I can call them that, are all on Medicare or Mental Disability. (*Unseen by them, ROSENBERG stands in the archway wearing Chris' kimono.*) I'm at the end of something. I don't know what I'm going to do.

POLLY. (*With theatrical tenderness.*) I'm here now. (*Notices Rosenberg.*) I've been very naughty keeping you from your client. I think I'll take a nappy. I am emotionally depleted. Don't let me sleep too long, darling. (*SHE exits through the archway.*)

CHRISTOPHER. (*Extremely tense. Up and crossing left to up left and retrieving his lab coat that's on a hook behind front door.*) Mr. Rosenberg, you've been very patient. (*Putting on the coat.*) I'm going to give you this session free of charge.

ROSENBERG. (*Crossing to just below right of sofa.*) That's not necessary.

CHRISTOPHER. (*Crossing back down to coffee table and opening it, HE takes out a pair of rubber gloves.*) I may not have a life, but I do have my principles. Please, get in that chair. (*ROSENBERG begins to sit in the chair.*) On all fours! (*ROSENBERG climbs into the chair on his hands and knees. As CHRIS puts on his rubber gloves, HE mutters to himself.*) She has some nerve, barging in here ... telling me what to do.

ROSENBERG. I feel like a collie at the dog show.

CHRISTOPHER. (*Humorlessly.*) Shoulders down. Raise your haunches.

ROSENBERG. Maybe we should do this some other time. You seem a little *fetutzed.*

CHRISTOPHER. (*Crossing right to just above chair.*) I am not *fetutzed.* I am a professional eyeing you with cold objectivity. (*HE flips light switch on wall just below archway.*) Now, we'll find a small area of flesh to experiment on, in case it burns. (*HE grabs electrolysis goggles that are hanging just below cabinet.*)

ROSENBERG. I think you've got something else on your mind.

CHRISTOPHER. (*Putting on the goggles and grabbing the electrolysis needle just inside the cabinet.*) Mr. Rosenberg, I am a licensed depilatory technician. Now lift that kimono. We will experiment on the buttocks.

(CHRISTOPHER raises his needle. MR. ROSENBERG looks terrified.)

BLACKOUT

ACT I

Scene 2

Several weeks later. Early evening. POLLY is standing in the middle of the room wearing a beautiful ball gown. SHE crosses down left to mirror on wall. The sound of a BLOW DRYER is heard offstage.

POLLY. Christopher, hurry! *(Crossing directly up, then right to archway.)* Flavia and Leonce will be here any minute. Forget the shoes. *(Crossing down right.)* This gown is so long. No one will even see my feet. *(SHE picks up a matching shawl from barber chair and puts it on.)*

CHRISTOPHER. *(Offstage.)* Be patient. You're going to be ecstatic. I promise you.

POLLY. I shall be extremely cross if I'm late for the Rainbow Room. No, really, darling, stop blow drying those pumps. I'm going barefoot. It's a charity ball for the homeless. It'll make a statement. *(To herself.)* I wonder if I should wear any rings. No, girl, keep it simple.

CHRISTOPHER. (*Entering with the matching satin pumps and crossing down right, just left of Polly.*) Here they are.

POLLY. (*Dropping shawl back on barber chair.*) How'd they come out?

CHRISTOPHER. (*Showing them to her.*) Darling, you'd never know that they were once psychedelic green. (*Putting them on the floor and helping her into them.*) They're still slightly damp.

POLLY. Ooh squishy. I feel like an extra in "The Poseidon Adventure." My God, this dress is divine.

CHRISTOPHER. It really costs six thousand dollars?

POLLY. Claudio Perucci is a major designer and frighteningly heterosexual. What your poor sister had to endure to borrow this rag. Now if I can just navigate past old Norma's door without her spitting at me.

CHRISTOPHER. She couldn't do that. She's completely paralyzed.

POLLY. Her spitting has the accuracy of a Scud missile. You know she loves you and hates me.

CHRISTOPHER. You're just paranoid because of that silly gift she gave you.

POLLY. A tiny coffin with my wax effigy. (*The INTERCOM buzzer goes off. POLLY crosses up around sofa to it.*) It's Flavia. Wouldn't you know ... for once she's prompt. (*SHE answers it.*) Sweetness, is that you?

FLAVIA. (*On the intercom.*) It's Flavia, darling.

POLLY. (*Into intercom.*) I'll be right down.

CHRISTOPHER. You really look great. (*Crossing right, then up to archway.*) Let me take a picture. Where's the camera?

POLLY. (*SHE crosses left and down to just above desk.*) Sweetness, there's no time. You've turned me into a princess. (*Looking through her purse on desk.*) Let's see, have I got everything? Lipstick, compact, keys, joints, condoms—where's my lucky rabbit's foot? (*SHE discovers it on desk, putting it in purse.*) Darling, I wish you could come. (*Crossing to up center, in front of door.*)

CHRISTOPHER. The last thing I'd want to do. (*Crossing to her.*) Remember every detail and tell me about it in the morning. (*Embracing her.*)

POLLY. It shan't be too early. Good-bye, darling. (*SHE opens the door and exits with a flourish.*)

CHRISTOPHER. (*HE sees her earrings on sofa table. Calling off:*) Polly, your earrings!

POLLY. (*Returning.*) It would serve me right if I forgot the damn things. (*Kisses him on the cheek.*) Love you. *Au revoire, mon frère.* (*SHE strikes a pose in the doorway.*) *Je vais à la gloire!* (*Exits.*)

(*CHRISTOPHER sighs and looks around at the empty, still room. The INTERCOM buzzer goes off. HE runs to the intercom.*)

CHRISTOPHER. (*Into intercom.*) Polly, what did you forget?

ROSENBERG. (*Over intercom.*) It's Sy Rosenberg.

CHRISTOPHER. Oh. (*HE buzzes him in, turns and notices that Polly has left her matching shawl on barber chair.*) She forgot her shawl. (*HE runs to the down left window, opens it and calls to her.*) Polly! Polly! (*She's gone. HE crosses to the shawl, picks it up, and stands for a minute, transfixed and mesmerized by its elegance. The DOORBELL rings. CHRISTOPHER drops the shawl on the window seat down, crosses up left to door and lets Mr. Rosenberg in.*) Good evening.

ROSENBERG. (*Entering.*) I saw your sister coming out the front door. She looked very elegant.

CHRISTOPHER. (*Closing door and following down left to window seat.*) We've done nothing for days but get her ready for this big extravaganza, and she left her shawl.

ROSENBERG. Oh, yes. Tonight's the charity ball for the M ...

CHRISTOPHER. (*Crossing in to Rosenberg.*) Metropolitan Coalition for the Homeless. Everyone's going to be there.

ROSENBERG. Except you and me and the homeless. Do you mind?

CHRISTOPHER. You couldn't drag me to something like that. It sounds hideous. I have this fantasy of what a glamorous ball should be like, something out of Proust or an MGM musical. Somehow, I don't think this one could compare.

ROSENBERG. Maybe not. (*ROSENBERG takes off his suit jacket and hands it to Christopher.*) Damn it, I forgot. I wanted to bring you some real hangers. (*HE sits *down wearily on the sofa.*) I'm forgetting everything these days.

CHRISTOPHER. (*Crossing left and up to hang jacket on a single metal hanger on a hook in the upstage window.*) You look exhausted. I don't mind canceling tonight.

ROSENBERG. No, I look forward to coming here. When Polly's not around, it's extremely restful.

CHRISTOPHER. Restful?

ROSENBERG. It's the conversation, Christopher. If it weren't for that, I think I'd give it up.

CHRISTOPHER. (*Crossing down to left of sofa.*) No. Your back and shoulders are almost as smooth as Harlow's. For only six weeks we've made great progress.

ROSENBERG. No one's going to see them.

CHRISTOPHER. (*Crossing up to just behind Rosenberg on sofa.*) You just had a rough day. (*Massages Rosenberg's shoulders.*)

ROSENBERG. I still miss Miriam so much. She's more real to me than my own daughter.

CHRISTOPHER. You still haven't called Lenore. You promised me.

ROSENBERG. Those lines of communication are closed.

CHRISTOPHER. What if I called her? I could tell her how much you needed her. I could say that you ...

ROSENBERG. Look, Christopher, that would only be a band-aid. The fact is that she doesn't like me and I know this is a terrible thing for a father to say but I really don't like her.

CHRISTOPHER. (*Crossing up around sofa to right and then down to behind barber chair.*) She must have some good points. (*Adjusting paper towel behind barber chair.*)

ROSENBERG. Lenore inherited her mother's legs and plastic surgeon. Chris, I'm a realistic man. No mumbo jumbo for me. But I want Miriam to haunt me. A tap on the window. Her breath on my cheek. I could live on that.

CHRISTOPHER. (*Crossing in to Rosenberg, sitting next to him.*) If you'd like, I could take out my Ouija board. Norma next door gave it to me. Norma once told me that children born at twilight like I was, have the power to even see spirits.

ROSENBERG. And have you?

CHRISTOPHER. Hmmm. A few months ago, I'd have put money down that I saw Hubert Humphrey at the D'Agostino. Should we try to contact Miriam?

ROSENBERG. Let the dead rest. If they could come back, we might not like what they have to say to us.

CHRISTOPHER. I used to wish my mother would haunt me. A couple of years after she died, I was sure I heard her voice and even caught a glimpse of her in the backyard. I've never seen my father although I've tried. (*Pause.*) It's probably a good thing that neither of my parents are floating around here. Polly and I haven't turned out to be exactly any parent's dream. Hey, would you like a drink? I think tonight we could both use a shot of bourbon.

ROSENBERG. (*With deep sincerity. Taking Christopher by the shoulders.*) You know something, kiddo? I think you're just great.

(CHRISTOPHER is startled by Rosenberg's sincerity. HE feels tears welling in his eyes and quickly pulls away.)

ROSENBERG. What's wrong? I've said something?

CHRISTOPHER. *(Getting up and starting to cry.)* Nothing. I'm so embarrassed. *(HE crosses right to just above barber chair.)*

ROSENBERG. Don't be.

CHRISTOPHER. Mr. Rosenberg, this may not be the best time ... I'm tired and ... I suppose I'm just relieved that Polly got off to the Rainbow Room. *(Starts to weep softly.)*

ROSENBERG. *(Getting up.)* Christopher, you are going to that ball.

CHRISTOPHER. Huh?

ROSENBERG. You heard me. *(Crossing left to desk and picking up phone.)* I'm going to make a few phone calls and you are going to that *forcockta* ball.

CHRISTOPHER. *(Crossing to him above coffee table and taking the phone out of his hands.)* Please don't. *(Crossing in front of Rosenberg and putting the phone back on the desk.)* If I was crying, it's because ... I don't know ... you've touched me in some way. Don't do this.

ROSENBERG. *(Crossing down below coffee table, then right.)* Why don't you want to go?

CHRISTOPHER. I'm pathologically shy.

ROSENBERG. You have no trouble talking to me.

CHRISTOPHER. I can only talk to Jewish senior citizens.

ROSENBERG. I hear Kissinger's going to be there.

CHRISTOPHER. I'm serious. Don't make me go.

ROSENBERG. I'm not going to force you to go. I wanted to do a good turn for you.

CHRISTOPHER. Why?

ROSENBERG. Why?

CHRISTOPHER. Why are you doing this?

ROSENBERG. Do I really need a reason?

CHRISTOPHER. I'd be interested in hearing one.

ROSENBERG. Well, I have the money to indulge myself and I'm in the mood to be extravagant. Does that make you feel better?

CHRISTOPHER. I don't know how I feel.

ROSENBERG. Could it be so extraordinary that I simply like you?

CHRISTOPHER. But you've known me for such a short time.

ROSENBERG. I'm a pretty good judge of character and believe me, you're a character. (*Sitting.*) I've never met anyone like you.

CHRISTOPHER. I'm not unique. There are thousands of us living in peculiar circumstances all over the village.

ROSENBERG. Then I should gather all of you together in the Javits Center. I'd have a helluva time. Look, I get a kick out of you. Must I explain? Chris, sit. (*CHRIS does so.*) You remind me of my father. Yes. Isadore Rosenberg. It's true. You see, my father was a dreamer. He invented the first collapsible suitcase thought he never made a cent from it. He was an immigrant, barely conversant in the English language. Had no business sense. He slaved all of his life at a bench in a factory. But he had a great dignity. It was always "Mr. Rosenberg," never "Izzy." The way we lived. On cold nights, all of us in one bed with our shoes on to keep from freezing, our stomachs rumbling from the eight of us having to share one small pullet for dinner. Hearing the cries of the Polish lady next door giving birth. But despite the hardships, my papa filled me with such wonderment. He could create magic with a phrase. The stories. How I wish I'd written them down. I'd forgotten how much I needed that magic. You cast the same kind of spell. So let me make a dream come true for you. What do you say?

CHRISTOPHER. It's all so complicated. What would I wear? I don't even have a pair of black shoes.

ROSENBERG. Easily solved. Next anxiety?

CHRISTOPHER. Socks, shirt, tie. Cuff links. You really could get me in?

ROSENBERG. One phone call. Judy Cunningham is a pal of mine. It's her charity. Look, I know I can be a steamroller. If you really don't want to go ...

CHRISTOPHER. I do want to go. I'd love to go.

ROSENBERG. Now he'd love to go. (*Getting up, crossing right and down around coffee table to left and finally, up to phone on desk.*) Then, kid, we've gotta get moving.

CHRISTOPHER. (*Getting up.*) What do I do?

ROSENBERG. Get yourself cleaned up. (*Clapping his hands.*) Go, go, go!

CHRISTOPHER. I'm going. (*Crossing right and up to archway. HE stops.*) I can't believe this is happening. (*HE exits into the archway.*)

ROSENBERG. (*Picking up the phone, crossing down to just below left of coffee table and dialing.*) Hello, this is Seymour Rosenberg. I'd like to speak to Mrs. Cunningham ... thank you. (*Pause.*) Judy, it's Sy Rosenberg. Dear, forgive me for taking you away from your guests. I'm sure you're all getting ready to leave for the Rainbow Room. I need to ask you a small favor ... No, I'm afraid I can't make it but I have a very dear friend, a young man, a protégé of mine and I'd like very much for him to attend.

(*The LIGHTS change. We hear MUSIC and the sound of a CLOCK ticking to indicate the passage of time. ROSENBERG crosses up stage center, making a new phone call.*)

ROSENBERG. Hello Morty, Sy Rosenberg. I hope I'm not interrupting your dinner. I'm in a bit of an emergency. I need one of your finest tuxedos. An Armani, something very distinguished and stylish and I need shoes, socks, shirt, cuff links, the works and I need it delivered in the next twenty minutes. Not for me, for a very dear friend. Well, it's like a fairy tale.

(*Once again, LIGHTS, MUSIC, TICKING. ROSENBERG crosses and sits at desk, making a new phone call.*)

ROSENBERG. Hello Chickie, Sy Rosenberg. How are ya? Look Chickie, I need a car sent over in a half hour. Not the usual. Something wonderful. Have you got a white Rolls? Perfect. Bill it to me and send the car around to 312 Bank Street, just off of Bleeker. Apartment 2E.

(MUSIC and TICKING sound. The LIGHTS get brighter and it's now forty-five minutes later. CHRISTOPHER enters transformed. HE's wearing an elegant tuxedo and looks like a young prince.)

CHRISTOPHER. *(Entranced. Crossing down right.)* How do I look?
ROSENBERG. You're a very handsome young man. I don't want you to say anything. But I would like you to look outside that window.

(CHRISTOPHER crosses left to down left window and looks down.)

CHRISTOPHER. *(Astonished.)* Is that car supposed to ...
ROSENBERG. It's a white Rolls. A little vulgar, but it's fun. It's yours for the night. Enjoy.
CHRISTOPHER. And it won't turn into a pumpkin?
ROSENBERG. It never will. But, don't lose that shoe. It's a rental. *(HE crosses up right and puts on his coat.)*
CHRISTOPHER. *(Suddenly insecure. Crossing to desk, adjusting desk chair and turning off desk lamp. Then,*

crossing up center and turning off lamp on sofa table.) Mr.
Rosenberg, what if I ...?

ROSENBERG. You're gonna give your name at the
door. You're gonna walk inside, head up, back straight.
You're gonna look everyone in the eye and say to yourself,
"I have more wit, charm and intelligence than all of you."
You're gonna dance, eat and mingle. You've got your
keys? You've got cash?

CHRISTOPHER. (*Very touched.*) Yes. I've got
everything.

ROSENBERG. You certainly do. Don't waste another
minute.

*(CHRISTOPHER opens the front door. MR.
ROSENBERG exits. CHRISTOPHER turns off light
switch on wall just right of door. Overcome with
emotion, HE stands for a moment in silhouette, then
exits.*
LIGHTS FADE.)

ACT I

Scene 3

*POLLY is discovered on the telephone at the desk stage
right.*

POLLY. Darling, please don't be so upset. I feel awful
about it. Claudio, just calm down. Of course, you know

the dress made a complete sensation. I'm sure the Times will run a photo in the Style section ... I know, I know, I know I promised to return it today, but I just can't. Now stop that. You know that I am the most responsible person in the world. For God's sake, I take care of my invalid aunt. I know what responsibility and obligation mean. (*Calling off to an imaginary aunt.*) Aunt Rose, do be careful with that walker. Don't overdo it. Nurse, would you please ... Claudio, it's just madness here. (*The INTERCOM buzzes. POLLY crosses to it, buzzing in Rosenberg downstairs.*) No, no. Claudio, you can't send someone over for the dress, because I'm not even home. I'm in Paris. Yes, yes, it is a very good connection. I'm afraid I won't be back for at least a week. Darling, I really must run. Our guide is here. We're taking a private tour of Versailles. You know, all the little rooms that have been locked up since the revolution. Le Petit Trianon and everything. (*The DOORBELL rings. SHE opens the door and lets Rosenberg in.*) Excuse me, Claudio. (*POLLY strategically places down the phone and motions Rosenberg to be quiet.*) Un moment, monsieur, je suis à la telephone avec mon coutouriere en Amerique. (*Picking up telephone.*) Claudio, you can see I'm just frantic. I'll call you as soon as I return. Bless you, darling. (*SHE hangs up. Then, to Rosenberg:*) Well, if it isn't the Scarsdale fairy godfather.

ROSENBERG. Good afternoon, Polly.

POLLY. Your friend, Cinderella, is visiting the old crone next door and will be home shortly. May I get you some coffee? We're running a bit late today.

ROSENBERG. No, thank you. I'll just get changed. (*HE exits through the archway. From off.*) Were you surprised to see your brother at the Rainbow Room?

POLLY. (*Crossing to archway.*) Surprised is hardly the word. Contrary to rumor, I am not the wicked stepsister. I was thrilled to see Chris all dolled up and so downright vivacious. I can't thank you enough for doing this.

ROSENBERG. Did you have a splendid time?

POLLY. (*Crossing to and sitting on sofa.*) I don't know if I'd say "splendid." It certainly was fraught with drama. It was all so silly, really. This, um, gentlemen friend of mine lent me some pieces of his wife's jewelry for the evening. Well, I guess he hadn't told her and didn't realize she'd be there last night. Naturally, she recognized the jewelry and it all got rather ugly. Food flying. But, the good news is that the stain on the dress will come out.

ROSENBERG. (*Re-entering through archway.*) I'm sure it'll all be forgotten by tomorrow.

CHRISTOPHER. (*Entering through the door.*) Mr. Rosenberg, I hope I haven't kept you waiting. Please have a seat. I'll be right with you.

(*ROSENBERG sits in the barber chair. CHRISTOPHER grabs his lab coat and puts it on.*)

CHRISTOPHER. I was next door telling Norma all about last night. You should have seen her, Polly. I actually got her to put her dentures in. I swear she looks just like Agnes Moorhead. (*HE opens the electrolysis cabinet behind the barber chair.*) We really should get started. I'm not in a rush, but I met someone last night and he's coming over in a few hours.

POLLY. (*Overjoyed.*) You met your prince.

CHRISTOPHER. I don't know about that. He's a publicist. (*Crossing to, kneeling at, and opening the coffee table to remove an instrument and rubber gloves*.) He's quite young, but he's worked with everyone from Lainie Kazan to serial killers.

POLLY. (*Suggesting that there might've been more to Christopher's encounter.*) Mmm hmm?

CHRISTOPHER. Don't get excited, Polly. It was just a romantic night. I'm not getting married.

ROSENBERG. (*Sincerely surprised.*) You're a ... homosexual?

POLLY. (*Incredulously acid.*) Oh, no.

ROSENBERG. (*Embarrassed.*) Not that it's an issue. Not at all. I'm a liberal. I ... I ... It never occurred to me. There's nothing effeminate about you.

POLLY. (*Confused.*) We are talking about *my* brother?

CHRISTOPHER. (*Irritated.*) Yes, Polly.

ROSENBERG. (*Fumbling.*) Well, there's nothing to discuss. You're a gay. Big deal. Everyone has a right to ... Today, it's the "in" thing. *Angels in America.* Far be it for me to ... So, um, Chris, your new friend—is he handsome?

CHRISTOPHER. (*Amused. Up and crossing back to electrolysis cabinet.*) Uh huh.

POLLY. Is he rich?

CHRISTOPHER. I don't think so.

ROSENBERG. Is he Jewish?

CHRISTOPHER. Yes. (*HE turns on the electrolysis machine.*) His name is Walter Zuckerman. We hit if off and he's coming over later. That's really all there is to it.

ROSENBERG. (*Pleased.*) What a night you must have had.

CHRISTOPHER. It was perhaps the greatest night of my life. (*Crossing to and sitting on sofa.*) Here I was actually thinking of going back to Albuquerque, but, now, I never want to leave this warm, friendly, quaint little city.

ROSENBERG. Did you meet Judy Cunningham?

CHRISTOPHER. Oh, yes. She found me almost the minute I arrived and she introduced me to everyone. It was like I was wearing an enchanted tuxedo. Words just tumbled out of my mouth. (*To Polly.*) Darling, you've never seen such poise outside of a Constance Bennett picture. I spoke with Mario Buatta and Dina Merrill and, let's see, um, Spaulding Grey and Betty Comden—she was awfully nice, and Orson Bean. (*HE puts on the rubber gloves.*)

POLLY. My word.

ROSENBERG. You see, you can relate to people. Next time, it'll be even easier.

CHRISTOPHER. I'm not sure I can do it without the tuxedo. (*Up and crossing to Rosenberg.*) By the way, everything is packed and read to go back.

ROSENBERG. It's paid for. It's yours to keep.

CHRISTOPHER. You can't do that. It's too much.

(*ROSENBERG motions him to say no more.*)

POLLY. Isn't that marvelous. I don't suppose the Rolls is …

ROSENBERG. That went back.

(CHRISTOPHER removes a cotton ball and rubbing alcohol from the cabinet and begins to prep Rosenberg's neck and shoulders.)

POLLY. *(Stumbling to get out of an awkward situation.)* Oh, yes … I'm sure. I was just wondering … *(Sighs. Stands and crosses to the archway.)* Last night had a bit too much mad frenzy for me. Wake me up before the century turns. *(Exiting through the archway.)*

ROSENBERG. My, but it's close in here. Maybe you could turn on the air conditioner.

CHRISTOPHER. It is awfully fierce. *(HE crosses to the air conditioner.)*

ROSENBERG. I hope you have that thing serviced yearly. You don't want it to die on you during the hottest day of the summer.

(CHRISTOPHER turns on the old unit which rumbles to a start. The LIGHTS in the room dim. The air conditioner has created a power surge, altering the electrical output in the room. CHRISTOPHER returns to his work.)

ROSENBERG. This young man who's coming over. You really like him?

CHRISTOPHER. Sure, but it's just a first impression.

ROSENBERG. I'm a believer in first impressions. You two have similar interests?

CHRISTOPHER. Oh yes. He loves old movies. Especially *Women's Prison* starring Ida Lupino. (*HE takes the electrolysis goggles from underneath the cabinet and dons them.*) I always used to fantasize that she was my mother.

(*CHRISTOPHER removes the electrically charged electrolysis needle from the cabinet and begins to go to work. HE manipulates a foot pedal at the base of the chair which operates the pen. We hear the NEEDLE buzz twice. On the second buzz, every major LIGHTING FIXTURE in the room goes on and off individually. There is obviously something wrong with the electricity.*)

CHRISTOPHER. (*Matter-of-factly.*) The wiring in this building is so decrepit. You can't have too many appliances on at the same time. For instance, I can't simultaneously blow dry my hair, use a power tool and make toast. I'm afraid I'm going to have to turn off the air conditioner. (*HE grabs a paper towel from below the cabinet to protect his sterile gloves, crosses to the air conditioner and turns it off.*) The landlord keeps promising to rewire this building. (*HE crosses down to the second window and opens it.*) Sometimes, if I open this window, I get a good breeze from the river. Let's get cracking.

(CHRISTOPHER returns to Rosenberg, picks up the needle and starts to work again. We hear another BUZZ. ROSENBERG flinches.)

CHRISTOPHER. I'm sorry. Did you get a shock?

(Suddenly ROSENBERG gasps, has a heart seizure and collapses. HE is motionless and quite dead. CHRISTOPHER is oblivious to Rosenberg as HE stares at the needle to figure out the problem.)

CHRISTOPHER. That's never happened before. (*HE looks down and thinks that Rosenberg is pulling a prank.*) Mr. Rosenberg. Mr. Rosenberg? C'mon. (*Suddenly aware that something terrible has happened, HE begins to gently slap Rosenberg on the face.*) Mr. Rosenberg? Are you alright? Mr. Rosenberg? Polly! (*In hysterics, CHRISTOPHER exits through the archway. The following dialogue is heard from offstage.*) Polly! Come here quick!
    POLLY. What is it?
    CHRISTOPHER. It's Mr. Rosenberg. Something happened to him. He's unconscious. The electric current must have been too strong. He's had some sort of seizure.

(The TWO bolt through the archway, POLLY leading the way. SHE picks up Rosenberg's wrist, trying to detect a pulse. Then, SHE leans over to listen to his heart. Finally, SHE waves her hand in front of his face to detect breathing. CHRISTOPHER paces through the whole process.)

CHRISTOPHER. Is he alright? Of course he's alright.

POLLY. (*Dropping Rosenberg's arm in repulsion.*) He's dead.

CHRISTOPHER. (*Pushing her away and grabbing Rosenberg.*) No, he's not! Wake up. Wake up!

POLLY. His heart isn't breathing at all.

CHRISTOPHER. Don't say that. (*Near tears and feverishly slapping Rosenberg.*) Mr. Rosenberg, please, wake up!

POLLY. Chris, stop it! He's dead. This is no time for hysterics.

CHRISTOPHER. (*On the verge of hysteria.*) Polly, you don't seem to understand. I have executed another Rosenberg! I am a murderer!

POLLY. He was an old man. He never looked well. He most likely had a heart attack.

CHRISTOPHER. (*Realizing his loss, and kneeling beside Rosenberg.*) He can't be gone. I couldn't even say good-bye. I can't even say good-bye.

POLLY. You do have malpractice insurance, don't you?

CHRISTOPHER. I never got around to it. Oh, I don't care. I accept my punishment.

POLLY. There's only one thing for us to do.

CHRISTOPHER. What's that?

POLLY. Ditch the body. If we can squeeze him through the bathroom window, he'd fall into the air shaft. (*Crossing to stage left.*) We'll need alibis and good ones. I don't suppose your friend Orson Bean would take us in?

(*The INTERCOM buzzes. POLLY crosses up and answers it.*) Hello? Who's there?

WALTER. (*On intercom.*) Walter Zuckerman, Is Chris there?

CHRISTOPHER. Oh, my God.

POLLY. (*Into intercom.*) I'm sorry. My brother just stepped out.

(*CHRISTOPHER rushes to the intercom, pushing POLLY out of the way.*)

CHRISTOPHER. Walter, you're rather early.

WALTER. (*On intercom.*) No. We said three.

CHRISTOPHER. I thought it was four. Maybe you should come back later.

WALTER. (*On intercom.*) I'm having trouble understanding you. Someone's opening the door downstairs. I'll come up.

CHRISTOPHER. Oh, my God.

POLLY. Ditch the body!

CHRISTOPHER. No, no. We won't do that. I need time. Help me bring him over to the sofa. We'll lie him down there and cover him with throws and pillows. (*HE crosses down to clear the coffee table to stage right.*) I'll keep Walter distracted. We won't even let him into the apartment. Help me move him.

POLLY. He's a big man. My back's never recovered from that last *Nunsense* tour.

CHRISTOPHER. We've got to hurry. We need to clear all the pillows and throws off the sofa.

(In a mad frenzy, THEY pull everything off the sofa and then cross to either side of the body. The DOORBELL rings.)

CHRISTOPHER. Is that you, Walter?
WALTER. *(Through the door.)* It's me.
CHRISTOPHER. I'll be right there. *(To Polly.)* Now, let's flip him over gently like a crepe. *(Beginning to lift the body.)* Let's lift him up gingerly. Gingerly.

(THEY walk the body to the center of the sofa. All THREE fall backwards onto the sofa.)

CHRISTOPHER. You take his legs. I'll get his head.

(THEY position the body across the sofa. ROSENBERG's knees are bent. POLLY pushes down on them with one lunge and the body is perfectly placed. CHRISTOPHER starts draping the body with a velvet Victorian throw.)

CHRISTOPHER. Now, let's drape everything over him for a nice, casual effect.

(CHRISTOPHER starts heaving pillows at Polly. The TWO place colorful pillows all around and over the corpse to disguise its contours.)

CHRISTOPHER. Darling, that red one would look ever so much prettier beside the puce.

POLLY. This is silly.
WALTER. (*Offstage.*) Chris! Hello!

(*CHRISTOPHER dashes to the door, with POLLY at his heels. CHRISTOPHER realizes he is still wearing the lab coat. HE frantically takes it off. POLLY helps and hangs it up. CHRIS straightens himself and opens the door.*)

CHRISTOPHER. Here I am.

(*WALTER is a good-looking guy in his thirties. Somewhat neurotic, it doesn't interfere with his natural charm.*)

WALTER. I thought you forgot about me.
CHRISTOPHER. I certainly did not. (*HE ushers Walter in and closes the door.*) Walter, this is my sister, Polly.
POLLY. Hello, Walter.
WALTER. I have a feeling I caught you off guard.
CHRISTOPHER. I suppose you have. I … I … I was nude.
POLLY. So was I. We're nudists.
CHRISTOPHER. (*Regretting that line.*) Experimenting with it. It was our first time. Doubt we'll ever do it again. It's such a beautiful day. Polly, we're going for a walk.
WALTER. Must we? (*HE crosses right, down and around to the front of the sofa.*) It's so hot. On the radio, they said a schnauzer exploded on Third Avenue. Can we sit down?

(CHRISTOPHER crosses down and intercepts Walter's attempt to sit on the sofa, ushering him down stage left to a hideous, metal, straightback chair with a tiny triangular seat. It's more sculpture than chair.)

CHRISTOPHER. Of course. Why don't you sit over here. It's so much nicer.

WALTER. *(Sits with great effort. Sincerely.)* Gee, I thought this was an ashtray.

CHRISTOPHER. It's based on a sculpture by Giacometti.

(CHRISTOPHER and POLLY with nowhere else to sit, kneel just right of Walter.)

WALTER. Must you kneel? I feel like Hans Christian Andersen.

POLLY. *(Rising abruptly.)* I really must go. *(SHE crosses to the door and opens it.)*

CHRISTOPHER. I don't want to chase you out.

POLLY. You're not at all. I'll be right back.

CHRISTOPHER. But, you've got nothing on underneath that robe.

POLLY. So true. I suppose I'll try this nudist thing out on Mrs. Abbotelli on the front stoop. Lovely meeting you, Walter. 'Bye. *(SHE exits.)*

WALTER. You did want to get together today?

CHRISTOPHER. Oh, yes. *(Sits hesitantly on the farthest edge of the sofa.)*

WALTER. For a minute there, I wasn't sure. Since last night, I've thought a lot about you.

CHRISTOPHER. Same here.

WALTER. It's the strangest thing. I feel like I've known you for, I don't know, forever. It's like we can dispense with all the preliminaries of friendship and just be, you know, for real. Ask important questions. Have you ever been in love?

CHRISTOPHER. No.

WALTER. Have you ever been in therapy?

CHRISTOPHER. No.

WALTER. I guess these are dumb questions. Do you have a terrible fear of death?

CHRISTOPHER. (*Sprawling across the corpse, appearing more casual.*) Not as much as I thought. You get sort of used to it. What do you think about death? I mean *really* think about it?

WALTER. (*Crossing up left, around couch and then to archway, taking in the room.*) One of my first jobs when I came to New York was with The Daily News. I assisted the photographer who shot murder victims. After awhile, nothing shocks you.

CHRISTOPHER. (*Encouraged.*) Walter, I should explain something to you. Remember I told you I perform electrolysis on people? Well, I have this client, a wonderful man. He sent me to the ball last night just like ...

WALTER. (*Coming down to right of sofa.*) The girl with the glass shoe. That was his Rolls Royce?

CHRISTOPHER. He paid for it. I have a confession to make.

WALTER. He's your sugar daddy? That's cool. I'm not judgmental. My cousin Francine is a professional dominatrix.

CHRISTOPHER. ... skip it.

WALTER. Listen, I can't believe I told you all about my rotten childhood and therapy.

CHRISTOPHER. (*Rising.*) No, I find your neuroses absolutely fascinating. I really do.

WALTER. You don't think I'm just a spoiled, suburban Jew?

CHRISTOPHER. No. Please. I mean, that whole thing about your brother making you believe you were Filipino. That's hardly standard issue, suburban angst.

WALTER. Is that couch just for display, or can we actually recline on it?

CHRISTOPHER. (*Sitting nervously and fluffing pillows.*) A neighbor's cat shed all over the pillows. If you have any allergies at all ...

WALTER. (*Sitting on sofa arm right.*) I'm that rarity. A neurotic without allergies. (*HE sits next to Chris and nuzzles his neck.*)

(*Throughout the next speech, WALTER seduces Christopher, kissing his neck and finally pulling his left arm up and kissing it from top to bottom.*)

CHRISTOPHER. (*Guilt-ridden.*) Walter, I'd think twice about seducing me. My mother, who had a very *slight* drinking problem, fell out of her window while writing a poem. And my father, my father had his head bitten off while performing a Punch and Judy show at the zoo. I am dogged by bad luck.

WALTER. I love it. Tell me more.

(WALTER throws Chris' left arm around his neck and tackles him directly back on the sofa. The force of the tackle dislodges Rosenberg's arm from underneath the throw and pillows.)

CHRISTOPHER. Walter, please.

(CHRISTOPHER discovers Rosenberg's arm and is near hysteria. With WALTER on top of him, CHRIS pulls his body left to try to cover the hand. Unsuccessful, HE tries to stuff the hand underneath him. WALTER's head comes up. In a panic, CHRIS stuffs his own left arm underneath himself, while grabbing Rosenberg's hand with his right hand, making it seem as if Rosenberg's hand is his own.)

WALTER. Am I too heavy on you?
CHRISTOPHER. No.

(WALTER kisses down Chris' right arm to his hand and eventually kisses the dead hand. CHRISTOPHER is horrified.)

WALTER. (Nestling his head on Christopher's chest.) Your hand is cold.
CHRISTOPHER. And prematurely aged.

(WALTER continues his advances with fervor.)

CHRISTOPHER. Walter, stop. Stop!

(CHRISTOPHER pushes Walter off him and pulls the pillow away to reveal Rosenberg's face. WALTER screams in wild hysteria.)

WALTER. Who is this man?

CHRISTOPHER. Seymour Rosenberg.

WALTER. You killed him?

CHRISTOPHER. Possibly. If I did cause his death, it wasn't intentional. I was performing electrolysis on him and he died from a sudden heart seizure.

WALTER. We must call the police. This man needs to be buried. You weren't planning on keeping him here, were you?

CHRISTOPHER. Walter, I'm not a ghoul. I'm just an unlucky electrologist with a sense of whimsy.

WALTER. I'll call the police if you'd like.

CHRISTOPHER. *(Crossing to Walter in front of sofa.)* Thank you and thank you for sticking around. You really didn't have to. As a matter of fact, maybe you should leave. I've never killed anyone before, but for some reason, it seems indicative of my lifestyle. You shouldn't get involved. You didn't bring a jacket or anything, did you?

WALTER. What? Are you kicking me out?

CHRISTOPHER. I'm making it easy for you.

WALTER. What if I don't want to go?

CHRISTOPHER. Walter, look at me. Look at the way I live. It's not romantic. It's pathetic. This mess. Dust everywhere. Woodwork half stripped. Fresh cadaver.

WALTER. So?

CHRISTOPHER. (*Starting to open door.*) It was wonderful meeting you, Walter.

WALTER. (*Spinning Chris around and holding him by the shoulders.*) I don't think you understand where I'm coming from. I'm attracted to you both physically and morbidly.

CHRISTOPHER. What?

WALTER. It's situations like this that made me want to move to New York. I grew up in the San Fernando Valley for chrissakes. It's nothing but malls, suntan lotion and car washes. I crave darkness. You are dark. Lonely rooms at midnight, insane fantasies, the grotesque. You embody all this. I wanted to live on the edge and experience heightened emotions. This is our first date. Where can we go from here?

CHRISTOPHER. I would like to kiss you. Just once before the police arrive.

WALTER. Before the eyes of a dead man?

CHRISTOPHER. Yes, I think he would approve. (*HE begins to advance left, in front of the sofa, to Walter.*)

WALTER. (*Backing upstage away from Christopher.*) Please, Chris, not here. You're going too far.

CHRISTOPHER. (*Like a High Priestess.*) Kiss me.

WALTER. (*Backing up right toward archway.*) I'm a very defiant person. I really am. I'd kiss you anywhere else.

I mean it. At an army induction center, at Temple Emmanuel, at a Knicks game.

CHRISTOPHER. (*Advancing on him.*) Now.

WALTER. (*In terror. Disappearing into archway.*) Noooo!

(In a very melodramatic style, CHRISTOPHER parts the beaded curtain at the archway. A very loud ORGAN CHORD is heard.)

BLACKOUT

ACT I

Scene 4

One month later. Mid-afternoon. WALTER is discovered straightening up the room, feather duster in hand. HE restores the coffee table and arranges pillows back onto the sofa. POLLY enters through the archway wearing a short skirt and camisole, blouse in hand.

POLLY. (*Crossing down left, pulling out the ironing board that is hidden Murphy bed-style behind a mirror.*) This is utterly ridiculous. How is it possible that I can perfectly scan a Shakespearean text, yet I am unable to iron a simple blouse? I do so want to make a good impression on Mr. Rosenberg's daughter. I've ironed this seven times and look at it. As wrinkled as an elderly scrotum.

WALTER. Polly, all morning I've watched you torture that helpless garment. I cannot tell you how much I've wanted to rip that goddamned iron out of your hands and iron that thing properly.

POLLY. Darling, why on earth haven't you?

WALTER. I don't want to appear controlling. It's an issue I'm working on in my therapy.

POLLY. I won't tell a soul. Please, be my guest.

WALTER. (*Crossing down to her, dropping the feather duster on the sofa.*) Thank you.

(*HE grabs the blouse and pushes Polly center. HE takes the plugged iron from the desk behind him and begins to expertly iron. POLLY sits on the sofa table.*)

WALTER. It's the taking over part. I can feel myself turning into my mother. It's awful. I distrust every generous act. By being helpful, I am really saying, "Give me that thing. You can't do anything right, you little schmeggegie. I'm in control around here. Me! Me!" It's my mother, Evelyn Zuckerman, speaking. Suddenly, I'm wearing a metaphorical beige pantsuit.

POLLY. I had no idea. Well, I appreciate the gesture, no matter what the motive. I think you're the most perfectly divine brother-in-law.

WALTER. Shhh. I wouldn't use that term in front of you-know-who.

POLLY. You-know-who who's dressing in the next room? Oh, a little tension in the house of bliss?

WALTER. I wish there were. Chris and I have been seeing each other for a month now and I don't even know if he likes me.

POLLY. Oh he does. I know he's mad about you.

WALTER. Can't he just say I love you?

POLLY. Forget that. We don't say that sort of thing. Chris and I come from generations of cold, brittle sophisticates.

WALTER. I'm not like that at all. I have a great need to create a home with someone. A home that is stable, loving and nurturing. I know that alienates a lot of people. I'd love to be owned, manipulated, even exploited. It all sounds great.

(CHRISTOPHER enters carrying a tray of cheese and crackers. HE is wearing a madras sports jacket that's several sizes too small, a vest and chino pants from two different suits and a very peculiar tie. It is his idea of being "conservative.")

CHRISTOPHER. Saltines and Jarlsberg. Perfect.

POLLY. *(Matter-of-factly.)* Christopher, are you posing as a lesbian?

CHRISTOPHER. *(Placing the tray on the coffee table.)* How astute of you, Polly. I wish to project cool, no nonsense strength. This is, after all, my first meeting with the daughter of the man I killed.

WALTER. Stop that. *(Crossing down left.)* You were never charged with anything.

(The INTERCOM buzzes.)

POLLY. That must be the Stupacks.

CHRISTOPHER. *(Crossing to, and answering the intercom.)* Hello?

LENORE. *(On intercom.)* Lenore Stupack.

CHRISTOPHER. *(Into intercom.)* We're on the second floor. *(To Polly.)* Polly, please don't threaten the Stupacks with your unbridled sexuality.

POLLY. This outfit couldn't be more conservative.

WALTER. *(Crossing back up to left of sofa.)* Look, the poor woman is probably still in deep mourning. Both of you, be very sensitive and respectful. She's contacted you because she obviously feels some sort of bond ... *(Eyeing Polly's outfit.)* Polly, fix your blouse.

CHRISTOPHER. *(To Polly.)* I think the blouse you had on yesterday was ...

WALTER. Chris, check your fly. And the most important thing is to ...

(The DOORBELL rings. CHRIS goes to answer the door.)

WALTER. Answer the door.

(CHRISTOPHER answers the door. LENORE ROSENBERG STUPACK is a very stylish and very fierce suburban matron in her early forties. SHE speaks in a somewhat nasal New York accent, overlaid with pretension.)

CHRISTOPHER. Hello, I'm Christopher. Please come in. This is my sister, Polly and this is Walter Zuckerman.

WALTER. Good to meet you.

POLLY. So delighted. I've heard so much about you from your wonderful father. Please, sit down. Where is Mr. Stupack?

LENORE. For a half hour he's been trying to find a parking place for the LeSabre. I really can't stay very long.

CHRISTOPHER. I thought we could go for lunch. There are so many charming ...

LENORE. (*Abruptly.*) We brunched before we came into the city. (*SHE sits on sofa left.*)

WALTER. Did you father speak to you of his friendship with Christopher?

LENORE. No. Never. Not a word was ever uttered. This is all such a surprise to me. (*To Chris.*) I understand you were performing electrolysis on him?

CHRISTOPHER. (*Sitting on barber chair.*) Yes. He started out as my client, but we became close friends.

LENORE. I was going to wait until my husband got here, but he could take until the millennium to find a parking spot in this neighborhood. Let me get to the point.

CHRISTOPHER. Please.

LENORE. Shortly before my father passed on, he made a rather startling change in his will. It's stated that half of his estate, adding up to ten million dollars after taxes, should go to this completely unknown person, a person with no blood ties and no previous history. Ten million dollars, that, by all rights, should go to his only child, Lenore Marjorie Rosenberg Stupack.

CHRISTOPHER. How awful. So, you've come to find out who this person is.

WALTER. (*Crossing to Chris up and behind sofa.*) They know who it is.

CHRISTOPHER. Well, who is it? Is it someone I know?

LENORE. (*Losing all poise. Getting up.*) It's you!

POLLY. (*Gasping, screaming and reaching across sofa to Christopher.*) Ah ... Ahh ... Ahhhh!!

CHRISTOPHER. Me? I'm the ... I've inherited ten mil ... ten million dollars. To think that Mr. Rosenberg wanted to protect me. That he cared so much about me. I can't believe it.

POLLY. (*Sobbing. Crossing to Chris and kneeling.*) Chris, all the terrible things that have happened to us all our lives have paid off. (*Rising.*) My brother is such a good person, in some ways a saint. The good deeds he does for people, the sick, the lame.

CHRISTOPHER. (*Rising and crossing down center.*) We won't be selfish. We'll make great gifts to charity. We'll cure AIDS. We'll save the American Ballet Theatre.

LENORE. Perhaps I haven't made myself clear ...

CHRISTOPHER. (*Crossing to Lenore.*) Let me ask you just one question. Did you get the other half of the estate?

LENORE. Well, yes, of course, but ...

CHRISTOPHER. Oh, I'm so relieved. I know you and your father had your problems, but he'd never be so cruel ... Lenore, it would mean so much to me if we could embrace. I think your father would want that. (*HE reaches out to her.*)

(*CHRISTOPHER has fully embraced her. SHE struggles and throws him back to the sofa.*)

LENORE. Get off me! What is this? A mind game? Is this how you bamboozled my father? Well, you may have swindled a sick old man, but I've got news for you. My husband, Leonard, is an attorney with Mossberg, Lieberman, Melnick, Fein, and Glick. They'll fucking destroy you!

CHRISTOPHER. (*Sitting on sofa.*) Oh, dear.

LENORE. We find the contents of my father's alleged last will and testament to be completely and utterly unacceptable. (*Calming down, picking up a valise she had placed on the coffee table and crossing to the desk.*) I'd like to have waited for my husband but in this neighborhood, he's probably been mugged and/or verbally abused. (*Opening valise and pulling out an official looking document and pen.*) At any rate, I've got a document here for you to peruse and sign. It's a renunciation waiver. (*SHE hands it and a pen to Christopher.*) Sign beside the red arrows.

WALTER. A renunciation waiver? That means that he renounces all claim to his inheritance.

LENORE. This is correct.

POLLY. Chris, you don't have to sign anything.

CHRISTOPHER. (*Reading.*) "I renounce all claim to …"

(An other-worldly SOUND is heard. The ghost of ROSENBERG appears extreme up center. HE looks much the same as he did in life, perhaps a bit more pale, but still in the same three-piece suit.)

ROSENBERG. (*Crossing to behind sofa.*) Christopher, put down that pen.

(CHRISTOPHER turns completely up stage and sees Rosenberg. HE turns back to us in horror. Beyond shock, a silent scream overtakes him. HE crawls down from the sofa to behind Polly and Walter.)

POLLY. (*To Lenore.*) Look what you've done. My brother is a very fragile creature.

CHRISTOPHER. (*Pointing to Rosenberg.*) Polly, what do you see over there?

POLLY. (*Unable to see the ghost, SHE sees a portrait on the wall behind him.*) Just that depressing portrait you painted of me with my old nose.

LENORE. This entire affair is extremely painful for me.

CHRISTOPHER. Polly, squint your eyes and try to …

ROSENBERG. How the hell did I get here? Suddenly there was a whoosh and down the hatch I went.

CHRISTOPHER. Can anyone else see you?

WALTER. What?

ROSENBERG. Lenore! Polly! Hello? (*Crossing to Chris.*) I think only you have the pleasure of my company.

CHRISTOPHER. Walter, do you think a mind can really snap?

WALTER. Don't worry. We're going to work this out.

ROSENBERG. I'm glad to see it's working out with your friend.

CHRISTOPHER. Oh, Walter is very ...

WALTER. Chris, I'm right here.

ROSENBERG. Don't answer me. They'll think you're meshuga. (*Urging Chris to sit on sofa. Sitting himself.*)

(*POLLY and WALTER, concerned about Chris, move up right to confer about his mental state.*)

ROSENBERG. Chris, I don't know what I'm doing here, but I do know that I want you to have that money. I think you could do great things with ten million bucks for yourself and others. So, don't you dare sign that waiver.

LENORE. I'm sure we can all part as friends.

ROSENBERG. That money is yours. Say it.

CHRISTOPHER. (*Tentatively.*) This money is mine?

POLLY. Chris!

CHRISTOPHER. (*Stronger.*) This money's mine. (*Convinced.*) This money's mine. He wants me to have it.

LENORE. This means war.

ROSENBERG. Rip it up. That'll really frost her.

CHRISTOPHER. (*Picking up the document and crossing to Lenore.*) And further more ... (*Ripping up the paper.*) This is what you can do with this document, or should I rip it up smaller so you can use it by the sheet.

ROSENBERG. I like that.

LENORE. How dare you! How dare you!

CHRISTOPHER. Lenore, your father and I had a very special communication between us. He's still so vivid to me that I'm seeing visions of him like Our Lady of Fatima.

ROSENBERG. I hadn't thought of myself that way.

CHRISTOPHER. Stop it! I can't take it anymore!

LENORE. (*Taking a step toward him.*) You're buckling under 'cause you know you're a fraud. You never knew my father and do you know how I know you never knew him? Because my father was not a kind man.

CHRISTOPHER. He was very kind to me.

LENORE. My father was a controlling, tight-fisted man of business. All my life he showered me with presents: the prettiest pink party dresses, my own pony, a speed boat called "The Lenore." But, in the department store of his heart, there was no merchandise. The floor was empty. Nothing I could do was right. He didn't approve of my bas mitzvah performance, nor my choice of college sorority. Not even my choice of husband. Not one of my houses, not a one. Not a one of my houses would he approve of. All I wanted was a simple, "Lenore, the house, the ground ... beautiful. Honey, you done good." But no. You know what I got? "The trellis needs pruning." The trellis needs pruning? That was my father. The man was ice. I could've been dying of cancer and he'd say, "The trellis needs pruning." My father ... my father. I was an asthmatic child. Twice, I nearly died. Was my father at my bedside? No. Where was the man? On the phone, talking to his broker. Twenty-seven years of intensive psychotherapy, acupuncture, scalding baths, and the efforts of a German woman in Jersey City who sticks chopsticks up my nose—twenty-seven years of torture has taught me that my asthma was psychosomatically induced! My father was literally strangling the breath from my body! I had to scream at the gestalt therapist, "Daddy, let me breath! Let me breath!" And you have the temerity to imply that I didn't know my father?

ROSENBERG. (*At a loss.*) The trellis needed pruning.

LENORE. I knew my father damned well!

ROSENBERG. (*Sincerely.*) I know that I made some mistakes, but I loved that child.

LENORE. I am owed those monies.

WALTER. I think you should talk to our lawyer ... when we get one.

LENORE. I will have you know that I will contest this will to the bloody end. We were prepared to make you a settlement of ten thousand dollars. Oh, yes. But, now, you know how much you'll get? Bupkis. My husband works very closely with the District Attorney. Leonard will give him a call and the D.A. will reopen this case. We always suspected there was something fishy going on around here.

WALTER. The police cleared Chris of all charges.

LENORE. Believe me, the D.A. won't find it hard in convincing a grand jury to indict the electrologist here, of murder.

CHRISTOPHER. Murder?

ROSENBERG. Take the gamble.

CHRISTOPHER. The gamble.

LENORE. The lies you must have fed him. And then, the cold, calculating act of murder. Electrocution? You fried my father!

POLLY. You have said quite enough, Mrs. Stupack. You don't know how many times I heard my brother trying to convince your father that you weren't a selfish, money hungry bitch!

CHRISTOPHER. Polly, don't do this.

POLLY. Someone has to tell her. My brother even had the ridiculously sentimental notion of trying to bring you and your father back together again.

LENORE. Don't talk to me. I know all about you. Judy Cunningham told me what a whore you are. She told me that Sylvia Tannenbaum's son literally tossed your clothes out the window to get rid of you. And I know you screwed Rita Landman's husband, Murray, in the men's room of Tavern on the Green.

(POLLY slaps her across the face. LENORE is stunned.)

ROSENBERG. (*Sadly.*) My foolish girl.

LENORE. You are looking at an assault charge. (*Wildly.*) Where is my FUCKING HUSBAND? You and your brother are going to need a good lawyer.

WALTER. (*Crossing to door.*) Mrs. Stupack, this has gone on far too long. I think you should leave.

LENORE. With pleasure, fag! (*Crossing to pick up her valise on the desk, SHE stops. To Christopher, right below desk.*) Murderer! (*Back up to door, SHE stops. To Polly.*) Whore!

(LENORE exits. WALTER closes the door.)

POLLY. No matter how much you tip the attendant, they always tell. *(SHE collapses on sofa in tears.)*

ROSENBERG. I am deeply ashamed of the fruit of my loins. Chris, everything's going to work out.

CHRISTOPHER. Please, go away. *(Crossing to down right.)* Go away? You're not even here. You're a very bad migraine. *(Sits in barber chair.)*

POLLY. Oh, thanks. Kick me while I'm down, why don't you.

WALTER. Stop this, both of you. I've got an idea. *(Crossing down right to between Chris and Polly.)* We're going to fight this with the best weapon I have. Publicity.

POLLY. *(Perking up.)* Publicity?

WALTER. The Stupacks could kill us in court. We need a public outcry. We need to humiliate them with their own greed. I can create this in the media. This is a great story and I could get you a ton of publicity. That's my job.

ROSENBERG. *(Excitedly.)* This guy's on the ball. Listen to him.

POLLY. Talk shows. We'd be great on talk shows.

ROSENBERG. This is terrific!

CHRISTOPHER. I couldn't do that. I was too shy to raise my hand in class. I was even pee shy.

WALTER. I promise you, Chris, you won't have to pee on *Geraldo.*

ROSENBERG. Kid, you gotta stay in the game.

CHRISTOPHER. (*Wildly.*) Can't any of you see that there's a ghost in this room?

(*WALTER crosses to left in disgust.*)

POLLY. (*Angered.*) Chris, I swear. If you bring up Mommy and Daddy one more time ... (*Rising.*) Bury the dead. Get on with your life. Think of that goddamned amaryllis and bloom, Christopher, bloom!

CHRISTOPHER. (*Getting up and crossing left to center of couch.*) No talk shows. I'll tell you that right now. No talk shows.

POLLY. (*Crossing to his right.*) I'll teach you everything I know about being fabulous.

WALTER. (*Crossing to Christopher's left.*) You're perfect the way you are. The entire country's going to have a love affair with you.

CHRISTOPHER. That sounds fatiguing.

(*The THREE sit simultaneously, on the couch, chattering on about hatching their plan. ROSENBERG, not about to be left out, sits perched on the back right of the sofa, offering his advice. MUSIC builds as LIGHTS FADE.*)

END OF ACT I

ACT II

Scene 1

*Christopher's apartment, two days later. CHRISTOPHER
enters through the front door, carrying a large laundry
basket and keys. MR. ROSENBERG follows him into
the apartment. CHRISTOPHER puts the basket on the
sofa table just above the sofa. HE puts the keys on the
table and removes laundry detergent from the basket.*

CHRISTOPHER. I don't mean to appear ungrateful,
but you must see that since you willed me that ten million
dollars, my life has become a complete and utter shambles.
(*HE crosses to supply cabinet up left.*) And I don't even
have the money yet.

ROSENBERG. I wish you'd listen to me. Miriam
always had the girl separate the brights from the darks. It
makes a difference.

CHRISTOPHER. (*Crossing back to basket.*) I know
you meant well, but did you really think that Lenore would
just hand over ten million dollars? (*HE begins to put
laundry away in chest behind him.*)

ROSENBERG. You'll get the money. Button that top
button before you put it away.

CHRISTOPHER. Mr. Rosenberg, death has given you
a laissez-faire attitude. Shortly, I shall be defending myself

before a grand jury. Your daughter has teams of lawyers out to discredit me. She is implacable. Rumors abound that she intends to link me to the death of Marilyn Monroe. Walter thinks that the only way I can beat a murder rap is to become a celebrity. I am a terrible interview. That reporter from the Harrisburg Queer Weekly said that I was the weirdest thing he'd encountered since the Love Canal. (*CHRISTOPHER crosses to desk. Picks up sewing basket and large square of black fabric. HE crosses downstage and kneels on the floor. HE is pinning a hem on the fabric.*)

ROSENBERG. I understand your anxiety, but think for a moment what I've been through. That long walk towards the golden, blinding light. Had I only brought Raybans. And then, being reunited with all my dead relatives, each one with an ax to grind. Some serenity. You should have seen my Aunt Ida and her *verbisseneh* face, "Sy, where's the pressure cooker you promised me?" (*Under his breath.*) I'll give you a pressure cooker, you b ... (*Noticing Chris.*) May I ask what you're making?

CHRISTOPHER. Slip covers for Norma's memorial service.

ROSENBERG. The old woman next door. (*HE sits in barber chair.*) Now, she was old. I was taken cruelly, years before my time, but that old dame had it coming.

CHRISTOPHER. Still, she didn't desire to die like that. I keep replaying the events over and over and I don't think I'd do anything different. The electricity was screwed up again, so I re-plugged all the extension cords. All I did was turn on the microwave and her craft-a-matic chair flung forward, hurtling her over the credenza.

ROSENBERG. And that triggered a massive stroke. You had nothing to do with it. Not really.

CHRISTOPHER. I can't help feeling responsible. Anyway, as far as we know, she had no family. A few of us thought we'd have a small memorial service for her at the take-out place she ordered from. I thought covering the banquettes with black slip covers would give the Szechuan Palace some much needed ambiance.

ROSENBERG. What a kid. Always with the good deeds. I had to reward you. You see, Chris, when Lenore was growing up I used to say, "Of course, I'm not the best father. What do I know from little girls, but, ah, a son! That would be different." This miracle that I've come back, don't you see, it's my second chance.

CHRISTOPHER. Your what?

ROSENBERG. My second chance to be the father I always wanted to be. Everything you've told me about your childhood, your parents dying so young, it breaks my heart. I wish I could have been your dad. I would have taken you camping in the woods. Shown you how to pitch a tent and catch a fish.

CHRISTOPHER. Mr. Rosenberg, I appreciate your interest, but I wasn't that kind of child at all. I would have been miserable.

ROSENBERG. I'm sure you were a wonderful child. No parent couldn't have loved you.

CHRISTOPHER. I was very creative. When I was six years old, I started my own modern dance troupe. My big fantasy as a child was to be Susan Hayward in *I Want to Live*. How many times Polly and I would take turns going to the gas chamber. One day she'd toss the pellets, the next day I.

ROSENBERG. Christopher, I want … I want us to communicate.

CHRISTOPHER. But, we are. We've talked so much. My uvula has never had such a workout.

ROSENBERG. A father and son should have no secrets. Christopher, you haven't always been so forthcoming.

CHRISTOPHER. I must confess, I find it hard talking about myself and particularly about my sexual orientation. (*Crossing with sewing to desk.*) I'm really very old fashioned.

ROSENBERG. But I need to understand. My experience with homosexuality is so limited. I blinded myself to it. I never saw that it was all around me. My own family. When I look back now I see. My cousin Philip. He never married. He designed women's lingerie on Seventh Avenue. Lived for thirty years with a hairdresser named Conrad. Spent six months a year in Key West. Wore a caftan one year to Rosh Hashanah. I never suspected. My Aunt Esther lived for years with a very masculine airline executive named Delores. Esther called her Dudley. My nephew Jason demonstrates Lancome products at Bloomingdale's. I never knew. But, I have this feeling that gay or straight, I've been sent here to help you become a man.

CHRISTOPHER. (*Unconsciously camp.*) But, darling, I am a man. I really am. (*Suddenly HE doubles over in pain.*) Ow. Oh, God.

ROSENBERG. What's wrong?

CHRISTOPHER. I don't know. I've got stomach cramps and oh, my head. (*Suddenly aware of something.*) There's a spirit in this room.

ROSENBERG. Yes, me.

CHRISTOPHER. No, another one and it's trying to get inside me. It's a man. I'm gonna let him in.

ROSENBERG. Are you sure you should do this?

(*CHRISTOPHER begins moaning and strange, HOARSE SOUNDS emerge from him. His face contorts. Finally, a LOUD GRUNT, an EERIE LIGHT CHANGE and the possession is complete.*)

ROSENBERG. Dear God, he's being possessed by an evil spirit, a Dybbuk.

(*CHRISTOPHER speaks in the voice of Rosenberg's dead brother, Sheldon.*)

CHRISTOPHER. (*As Sheldon.*) No, Sy, I am not a Dybbuk. It's your brother, Sheldon.

ROSENBERG. Shelly? What, are you crazy? Get out of there. Don't you hurt the boy.

CHRISTOPHER. (*As Sheldon.*) I'm not hurting the kid. He feels nothing. What the hell are you doing here, Sy?

ROSENBERG. I had unfinished business. The young man needed someone to guide him.

CHRISTOPHER. (*As Sheldon. Sarcastically.*) And you're just the man for the job.

ROSENBERG. Why shouldn't I be?

CHRISTOPHER. *(As Sheldon.)* You're a great success. The great Wall Street *macher.*

ROSENBERG. Don't talk to me.

CHRISTOPHER. *(As Sheldon.)* This Christopher business is all a charade. You never change, Sy. You think you're the great giver of gifts, but it's all for yourself. Checkbook love.

ROSENBERG. Checkbook love? All the financial help I gave you all of our lives. Keeping your business open after the fire. Your Mindy's wedding. Sending your Stacey to college.

CHRISTOPHER. *(As Sheldon.)* A junior college.

ROSENBERG. Her SAT scores were in the single digits. Miriam warned me you'd throw my good deeds in my face.

CHRISTOPHER. *(As Sheldon. Scoffing.)* Miriam.

ROSENBERG. What about Miriam? Are you saying that I wasn't good to my first wife?

CHRISTOPHER. *(As Sheldon.)* It was a show marriage. You treated her like a professional asset, like a very efficient fax machine. I was there in the next room when she was dying. I heard her lash out at you the invective. And now, you carry on about the great idyllic marriage. You're such a phony, Sy. Come back. Face your truths, face your family.

ROSENBERG. I'm not afraid of my family. I was a beloved figure.

CHRISTOPHER. *(As Sheldon.)* Well, I've got a message from your late cousin, Florence.

ROSENBERG. What's Florence got to say?

CHRISTOPHER. *(As Sheldon.)* Florence says, "Fuck you." You wanna hear from cousin Ruthie?

ROSENBERG. Who do you think you are, the ghost of Chanukah past?

CHRISTOPHER. *(As Sheldon.)* I gotta go. The kid's sending me back. *(An internal struggle.)* The kid's got some will power. Alright, I'm going.

(An abrupt LIGHT change. SHELDON has vanished. ROSENBERG rushes around sofa to left of Chris.)

ROSENBERG. Chris?

CHRISTOPHER. That was really horrible. I really dislike your brother Sheldon. I couldn't get him out. I feel raped.

ROSENBERG. With Sheldon, it shouldn't be so bad. He had a pecker this size. *(Holds up his pinky finger.)*

(The door flies open. POLLY and WALTER emerge with lots of shopping bags. POLLY crosses right, depositing hers at the barber chair, and then flinging herself on the sofa right. WALTER follows behind her, picking up her bags and exiting through the archway.)

POLLY. I am vanquished. We walked all the way from mid-town. My feet are as swollen as two puffed up brioches.

CHRISTOPHER. Don't you think it's a bit premature to go out on a shopping spree? We don't have the money yet.

ROSENBERG. You'll get the money.

POLLY. Darling, I needed a new dress to wear on *The Wanda Wang Show*.

CHRISTOPHER. You're going on *Wanda Wang*? That's fantastic, Polly. You are the perfect talk show guest. You'll love Wanda Wang. I watch her every afternoon. She's so warm and compassionate.

WALTER. (*Bursting back into the room and crossing to up center of sofa.*) Polly is going to be sitting demurely on the sidelines. You're going to be Wanda's guest next Thursday.

CHRISTOPHER. Me? Talk to that awful, vicious woman? Have you seen how she humiliates her guests?

POLLY. Chris, stop it.

WALTER. (*Crossing to Chris.*) Contrary to popular belief, it's not easy booking someone on one of these shows. This took epic schmoozing on my part. Polly, would you give me some zinc oxide for my lips? That's for all the ass kissing I did.

CHRISTOPHER. (*Kneeling next to sofa left.*) You don't seem to understand. I am poise deficient. In sixth grade, I was cast in the school play, *My Fair Lady*. Opening night, I was so nervous, my face swelled up like a Macy's balloon. Polly insisted on going on for me.

WALTER. That was nice of her.

CHRISTOPHER. You should have seen her Colonel Pickering. Please don't make me go on TV. I beg of you.

POLLY. (*Standing.*) I really can't take anymore of this Emily-Dickinson-Shield-Me-From-The-Lamplight crap. (*Crossing up right.*) I shall let you boys trash it out amongst yourselves. Chris, you reject everything! I am tired of giving, giving, giving! (*Exiting through archway.*)

CHRISTOPHER. (*To Walter. Sitting sofa left.*) Honestly, I'm very touched by all the effort you've made.

WALTER. I'm not all that upset. Just for a second there, I had this feeling of total obliteration.

ROSENBERG. He's very sensitive.

WALTER. Chris, this is my gift to you. The kind of exposure you can get on *Wanda* could keep this case from going to court. She's big. She's got a leg up on Oprah.

CHRISTOPHER. I would if I could, but I will fail miserably. I will be struck mute.

WALTER. Look, I'm not being completely selfless. You going on *Wanda* means a lot to me in many ways. I've never booked anyone on such an important show. Please don't make me look like an idiot and cancel. Do this for me?

CHRISTOPHER. Walter, why did you have to do this? I can't ... I can't. (*Rising and crossing down left.*) And I'm not going to be bulldozed into this.

WALTER. (*Rising.*) Bulldozed? Bulldozed? (*Crossing down to him.*) That is a word I use when I refer to my mother, Mrs. Evelyn Zuckerman. I have spent countless hours in therapy dealing with this issue. I really can't accept this criticism. (*Beat.*) Alright, I accept this criticism. Everything I do for you is only to make myself feel important. (*Stops.*) If that is true, do you know why I do that? (*Slumps on sofa arm right.*) To make myself feel less like an impotent, ineffectual failure. I am a third-rate press agent. The high point of my career is representing this year's Mr. Chippendales and then running to Waldbaums to buy him Gax-X. Do I ever get sympathy?

CHRISTOPHER. (*Crossing up to sofa left, opposite Walter.*) You've got it all wrong, Walter. I'm the failure in this duo. I'm such a failure, homeless people don't even harass me.

WALTER. (*Standing.*) I have no money. I live off credit cards.

CHRISTOPHER. (*One step right.*) I can't even get a credit card.

WALTER. (*One step left.*) My life is about photographers telling me to get the hell out of the way.

CHRISTOPHER. (*Wildly.*) I am a Diane Arbus photograph! I can see it hanging at the Whitney. (*Sitting, illustrating photograph.*) *Gay Electrologist With One Eye Closed.* I should kill myself it would make a better picture.

WALTER. Oh, you won't kill yourself, you're tough as nails. You don't need people.

CHRISTOPHER. Oh, I don't?

WALTER. I'm the one desperately seeking affection and getting kicked in the tuchus. I should take an overdose of Seconal.

CHRISTOPHER. I'm such a dope, I'd take an overdose of Tums and end up with a giant lump of antacid in my stomach.

ROSENBERG. Would you two stop?

WALTER. Just answer me this. What is my role in your life? Am I your pal, your lover, your fling or your publicist?

CHRISTOPHER. (*Painfully.*) I don't know what I want you to be. I realize that's unfair. (*With rising intensity.*) I can't be all things to all people: lover, brother, ghostbuster, electrologist and defendant! (*Crossing up and sitting at desk.*) All I know is I've got to finish these slip covers.

WALTER. I don't know what you're saying. (*Crossing to door.*) I've gotta get out of here. I can't stand confrontations.

CHRISTOPHER. (*Getting up and crossing up to left of Walter.*) No, no, no, no. *I'm* the one who hates confrontations. Other than Lobster Cantonese, confrontations are what you enjoy most. You just love to communicate. Why must everyone communicate?

WALTER. Don't worry about it. I'm turning off all five hundred channels. (*Exiting through door.*)

(*CHRISTOPHER, utterly frustrated, looks at Rosenberg, crosses down to sofa left, stops and collapses on sofa.*)

BLACKOUT

ACT II

Scene 2

*Panels have been pulled from both sides of the proscenium
to reveal; the set of* The Wanda Wang Show. *Three
chairs sit in typical talk show formation just left of
center. The entrance, a space between the two sets of
panels, is center. POLLY and WALTER are discovered
center.*

WALTER. I shouldn't be here. I'll just get Chris
nervous.

POLLY. Darling, you must be here. You're our
publicist. You know how shy we both are. We need a
spokesman.

WALTER. Polly, you shouldn't have called me and I
shouldn't have said yes.

POLLY. But, darling, this is your Napoleonic triumph.
You set this up.

WALTER. But, it was the Waterloo for my
relationship. How's Chris doing?

POLLY. I told him, just a little finger down the throat
and he'll feel divine.

WALTER. How'd you get him to appear on the show?

POLLY. It wasn't so arduous. I have my little ways.
Anyway, darling, by his appearing on the show, it's his
way of telling you he wants to make up. Make it easy for

him, will you? Apologize? Regret is such an attractive quality in a man.

(CHRISTOPHER enters. HE is visibly a nervous wreck.)

CHRISTOPHER. Hello, Walter. Despite our differences, I feel compelled to warn you about getting too close to that woman.

WALTER. Why is that?

CHRISTOPHER. She is evil. She'll go to any lengths to get what she wants.

WALTER. What did she do to get you here?

POLLY. It really doesn't bear repeating.

CHRISTOPHER. You know the doll I made out of dried yams? My favorite one?

WALTER. The one based on Gene Tierney in *Laura*?

CHRISTOPHER. She's holding it hostage and is threatening to turn it into Edward G. Robinson. I hate her. (*Crossing left to Polly.*) Maybe if I get the ten million dollars, you'll finally move out.

POLLY. Chris, you'll thank me for this in the end. If the media finds you sympathetic, I just know Lenore will drop her lawsuit. You will be a free man and we'll be very rich.

CHRISTOPHER. I just wish I had more confidence in myself.

POLLY. I have great confidence in you. Christ, this audience is composed of little, insignificant people with tawdry little lives. They'll identify with you. Just be yourself. My only bit of advice is not to wave your hands around. Come to think of it, don't use them at all. You'll seem effeminate.

WALTER. (*Crossing left, just right of Chris.*) Polly, you're going to make him self-conscious. My only suggestion since I do know something about this, not that I'm being in the least bit controlling, is be careful raising your eyebrows. Sometimes when you get excited, you come off like Carol Channing doing *Sunset Boulevard*.

POLLY. When I've done chat shows, I've also learned not to tighten my mouth. Pursed lips are so unattractive. And whatever you do, do not lick your lips. On television, it's magnified a thousand times. You'll look like a gay Saint Bernard. (*Gasps as SHE sees Wanda.*) Oh, there she is. There's our hostess, Wanda Wang.

(*WANDA WANG enters looking over the itinerary on her clipboard. SHE is a very attractive and stylish Asian woman in her late thirties. Like many flamboyant personalities, her off-camera demeanor is quite different. When she's not "on," she's really "off."*)

POLLY. (*Crossing right to Wanda.*) Hello.

WALTER. (*Turning abruptly.*) Hello. Wanda Wang.

POLLY. (*Very vivacious.*) Of course we'd know you. My God, they'd recognize your face in the middle of mainland China. (*Suddenly aware of her faux pas.*) I'm Polly Lawrence. This is my brother, Christopher Ladendorf and this is Chris' publicist, Walter Zuckerman.

WALTER. (*Defensive.*) I'm just handling this one appearance.

CHRISTOPHER. (*Equally defensive.*) I won't be needing a publicist after this.

WALTER. He's remarkably self-reliant. He doesn't need anyone.

CHRISTOPHER. Especially people who insist on taking over every element ...

WANDA. (*Crossing center and taking control.*) Hey fellas, time out! You, the sister, didn't they tell you that no family is allowed past that door and definitely, no press agents.

POLLY. I realize that, but coincidentally enough, I happen to know your assistant stage manager, Bob ...

WANDA. You've got three minutes, then vamoose.

CHRISTOPHER. You're very different from your TV persona.

WANDA. My image is my product and I put it right back on the top shelf when I close shop.

CHRISTOPHER. Then your perkiness is just an illusion?

WANDA. My inner self, my "secret child," she's perky. On camera, I delve into the well and draw forth that hurt little girl. Therefore on television, I'm not a phony, but in a sense, more real.

VOICE OVER. One minute, Wanda.

(*Banks of LIGHT turn on as the show is being readied to begin.*)

WANDA. I'm getting the signal. We're about to start. Chris' sister and flack, outta here! (*SHE crosses behind Chris and sits in the center chair.*)

POLLY. (*Crossing left and hugging Chris.*) Darling, you're going to be divine. Personality, it's in our blood.

WALTER. (*Pulling Polly away and exiting with her into the audience.*) Polly, go. Chris, good luck.

CHRISTOPHER. (*Sitting in right chair.*) Wanda, do you think there's time for me to run to the ...

WANDA. (*Grunting fiercely. Clenching her fists, staring straight out. Not unlike a quarterback.*) Fuck 'em, Fuck 'em, Fuck 'em! (*SHE straightens up and, like Mr. Hyde, SHE's transformed into her familiar, warm, intensely upbeat, public self.*)

CHRISTOPHER. You've delved into the well, haven't you.

WANDA. You bet I have. Chris, we're gonna have fun. You're gonna look into these eyes. They're not scary eyes. And you're gonna tell me the whole truth and nothing but.

VOICE OVER. Ten seconds.

WANDA. (*Getting up and pointing out for Chris.*) See that feller in that gorgeous, orange sweater? That's Mike. He's giving me the signal to start. (*SHE crosses to the entrance and hands off her clipboard to an unseen assistant.*) Here we go. (*SHE crosses back and stands in front of her center chair.*)

VOICE OVER. In five, four, three, two ...

WANDA. (*On the air. Looking into the camera.*) Imagine your millionaire father dies. His will is read and you learn that he's left half of his estate to an unknown, gay electrologist. Do you accept, or do you fight back? "Homosexuals Who Inherit Straight Bucks" today on *Wanda.*

(Wanda's theme MUSIC plays. CHRIS, in a last ditch effort, gets up and tries to escape. WANDA sits. SHE spots him, jumps up and grabs him just before he leaves. There is a short struggle before SHE finally places him back in his seat and then reassumes her position. MUSIC changes to just a steady rhythmic beating sound.)

WANDA. *(On the air.)* Seymour Rosenberg, a wealthy widower, began seeing a young man for electrolysis. Six weeks later, Rosenberg was dead from a massive coronary, perhaps triggered from an electric shock. The day before his death, he changed his will and left ten million dollars to the young man. Will the electrologist live in luxury with Rosenberg's millions? Or will he be charged with murder and spend the rest of his days in a maximum security prison. *(The sound of a CELL DOOR closing.)* With me is Christopher Ladendorf, the controversial hair remover. *(SHE sits. To Chris.)* Were you surprised by the contents of the will?

(CHRISTOPHER, true to his word, is struck mute. HE is painfully aware of all the advice given by Polly and Walter.)

WANDA. (*Coaxing him.*) But, you had a very close relationship with Mr. Rosenberg.

CHRISTOPHER. (*At last able to speak, albeit tentatively.*) In one sense, but um ... (*HE inadvertently licks his lips and is, once again, totally self-conscious. HE finds HE is unable to stop licking his lips.*) Yes, we were very good friends.

WANDA. (*As if dealing with a nut case.*) Yeah. How did Mr. Rosenberg first come to see you? Did he answer an ad?

CHRISTOPHER. (*Finally onto something he can discuss, HE abandons all advice and speaks normally.*) Mr. Rosenberg fainted outside my apartment, so I helped him inside. (*His arms begin to flail.*) Once there, he saw the before and after photos of my client, Miss Hilda Fernandez. (*HE becomes aware of his hands and tries to affect a butch demeanor and lowers his voice.*) And, so, um ... Mr. Rosenberg couldn't help but be impressed.

WANDA. I bet. Well, let's get right to another side of this. We have with us Mr. Rosenberg's daughter, Lenore Stupack.

(*LENORE enters on applause. SHE sits to Wanda's left.*)

WANDA. Lenore, when you first heard the contents of your father's new will, what went through your head?

LENORE. Wanda, it was as if wild jackals had ripped apart my spleen. Mr father ... I loved my father, Wanda. I was his little girl. (*Starting to cry.*) I can't ... it's still too soon.

WANDA. (*To Chris.*) Chris, I think it's impor ...

LENORE. (*Interrupting.*) You live your life, go about your business and then, suddenly, pow, out of the blue, you become a victim. I am a victim, Wanda. Garbed, perhaps in Ultrasuede, but a victim, nevertheless.

WANDA. You feel Christopher has plotted against you?

LENORE. From the get-go. From the moment my father stepped into that electrolysis parlor, this young man's had his eyes on one thing and one thing only, my father's wallet. This person has filched and plundered my father's final gift to me. And it's not the money that matters. It really isn't, Wanda. I want ... I want my memories back. This horror has made me doubt the veracity of my most precious memories. I weep at night. I wail. I swear they can hear me down the street. "Give me back my dad! Please, return him to me!"

(*The AUDIENCE bursts into applause.*)

WANDA. Chris, I think you're losing them.

CHRISTOPHER. Evidently. I need help.

LENORE. He brought this all onto himself. Greed. That is the modus operandi in this particular scenario.

(*ROSENBERG enters and stands behind Christopher.*)

ROSENBERG. Don't let them kick you in the ass. You're wearing that magic tuxedo and, boy, do you look sharp. Get in there, kiddo.

CHRISTOPHER. Lenore, I think you should have the money.

ROSENBERG. (*Crossing away, right.*) That's not what I meant.

CHRISTOPHER. After all, you were his only child. (*To Wanda.*) They were sort of on the outs, but, I think had he lived, they would have patched things up. I mean, really, how angry could he have been? He left her ten million of her own.

LENORE. (*To audience.*) And all of you should know that ten million in today's economy is a drop in the bucket.

CHRISTOPHER. My sister would like me to have the money. She should be rich. She has fabulous clothes sense and no clothes. It's just pathetic. I'd love to see her in *haute couture*, but it's not worth it, not with all this ugliness.

WANDA. Do you have any other family besides your sister?

CHRISTOPHER. Nope. Just us.

ROSENBERG. I was always a loner.

CHRISTOPHER. That may have been why Mr. Rosenberg identified with me. He felt very alone in the world.

LENORE. I resent this implication, I really do.

WANDA. (*To Chris.*) Tell us about Mr. Rosenberg. From your heart.

CHRISTOPHER. I only knew him six weeks. I know that sounds bad. I never told him I loved him. I have a hard time expressing myself that way. And he never told me he loved me. But I know he did. He thought I was wonderful. (*To the audience with great simplicity and sincerity.*) Can you imagine what it felt like to have a stranger come into your life who thinks you're absolutely unique? (*To Wanda.*) You think I'm just weird, don't you?

WANDA. (*To Chris.*) No, I don't. I understand what you're saying very well. (*To camera.*) I was a fat, little Chinese girl from Oakland. But, I had a teacher. An English teacher in the eighth grade, Mrs. Wu. She was the only person who would give that chubby little kid any encouragement. It certainly wasn't my mother. But, that's another show. Anything Wanda Wang has achieved is due to Mrs. Wu.

CHRISTOPHER. I always wanted a teacher like that.

WANDA. (*To Chris.*) Every child needs someone to tell them they're special. (*Having an apparent revelation.*) Oh, God. I'm going to reveal something that I've never said in public. (*To camera.*) Something so private. Something I've lived with in secrecy for so many years. I have only one kidney. It was removed when I was twelve years old. Ever since, I've had to wear an elasticized corset, because my back muscles were weakened from the operation. (*Slowly breaking down in tears.*) All my life, I've felt scarred and incomplete. (*To Chris.*) Chris, oh yes, I know what it's like to feel different. To be alone ... (*To camera.*) ... alone in your little bathroom in Oakland, desperately trying to urinate. And feeling where that second kidney ought to be. To be so utterly alone. But, gosh, it feels good to finally get this out. It feels damn good. (*To Chris.*) Chris, come here. (*SHE stands and gets him up.*) Give me a hug.

(The audience bursts into applause.)

CHRISTOPHER. *(Overcome with sympathy.)* I'm so glad I was here today. This is a classic *Wanda* show. Just like last season, when you revealed you'd had the chin implant.

WANDA. *(Genuinely touched.)* I'm very glad you were with me today.

(WANDA and CHRIS sit back down.)

LENORE. Wanda, congratulations on your admission of your kidney problem. I just want to say that maybe I read this young man wrong. It is possible that he didn't intentionally brainwash my father.

ROSENBERG. She's up to something. She's brainy. She's a Barnard graduate.

LENORE. *(To audience.)* I'm trying to see both sides. It's possible that my father, in his weakened mental state, developed a fondness for his depilatory practitioner. These things happen. We live in a strange world. But, is it fair to give this relationship the same ...

CHRISTOPHER. Objection! I object. Your father was definitely not in a weakened mental state. No. He was sharp as a tack. He'd come over for a session and we'd talk for hours. Then, as a total surprise, he sent me to the most glamorous charity ball. I was driven in a white Rolls Royce and felt like ... I felt like Audrey Hepburn in *Sabrina*. I can't believe I just said that. It sounded so queeny, but, oh, what the hell, I'll never be on TV again. (*With great giddy panache.*) Who cares? (*The audience applauds.*) Thank you. Now, I'm going to give you a little encouragement, Miss Wanda. I think you're every bit as good as Barbara Walters or Oprah or any of them.

LENORE. I totally agree. Wanda, you're remarkable. But, back to my father's very suspicious death …

CHRISTOPHER. (*Carried away.*) One kidney or no, you are no longer that ugly fat girl from Chinatown. (*The audience applauds.*) Thank you.

WANDA. (*Very vulnerable.*) Oh, Chris …

CHRISTOPHER. (*With great emotion.*) You're beautiful, talented, accomplished and very, very special (*To audience.*) … as every one of you ladies is, in your own fashion. (*To Wanda.*) Now, Wanda, give a hug.

(*CHRISTOPHER stands as does WANDA. SHE collapses in his arms. The audience bursts with applause. Wanda's theme MUSIC is heard. LENORE is beside herself that the show got away from her.*)

LENORE. Shameless! Shameless!

CHRISTOPHER. (*Genuinely touched and trying to compose himself, HE turns to the camera. Over theme music and applause:*) I think it's time we took a short commercial break. We'll be right back

LENORE. (*As LIGHTS FADE.*) I am the victim here. I am the victim.

(*LIGHTS FADE.*)

ACT II

Scene 3

A week later. Christopher's apartment. The yam dolls have disappeared. Some knickknacks and books have been cleared away. There's a packing box on the down left window seat. ROSENBERG and CHRISTOPHER are entering through the archway.

ROSENBERG. I keep reliving that TV show. You had such poise, such panache.

CHRISTOPHER. I couldn't have done it without you.

ROSENBERG. I salute your initiative, but you haven't even begun shopping for a house. That takes time.

CHRISTOPHER. I guess I'm just impatient to start my new life.

ROSENBERG. (*Taking a couple steps down.*) I tell you, there are some great advantages to being invisible. I wish you could have seen Lenore's face when the D.A. told her she didn't have a leg to stand on. Lenore was not a happy woman. Security had to forcibly evict her from the building.

CHRISTOPHER. I hate hearing things like that.

ROSENBERG. (*Crossing up right.*) The point is the fight is over. She's not contesting the will. Son, I've got a million ideas for us. First of all, I see a book. All about our friendship, something very personal, from your point of view. Don't get anxious, Chris, I'll dictate the whole thing to you.

CHRISTOPHER. You know, I sort of see my appearance on *The Wanda Wang Show* as, well, graduation.

ROSENBERG. (*Crossing down to right of coffee table.*) I'm not following you.

CHRISTOPHER. (*Tentatively.*) I was always under the impression that you came back to get me on my feet and you certainly have. I'm doing things these days I never dreamed of. I actually go to the movies now and I take the subway. What's left?

ROSENBERG. Are you giving me the heave ho?

CHRISTOPHER. Of course not. I'm so grateful for what you've done for me and I'm so proud to have been your protégé, but I think it may be time for me to go my own way.

ROSENBERG. I can't believe you're saying this. I guess I saw us as sort of a team.

CHRISTOPHER. Mr. Rosenberg, kids grow up and I'm definitely not a kid.

ROSENBERG. I agree, but not yet. Yes, you were a hit on that talk show and yes, Lenore got intimidated and dropped her lawsuit, but, Chris, ten million dollars is a lot to handle. You need my advice.

CHRISTOPHER. (*Taking books from desk and crossing down to box.*) I hired John Gerbner as my business manager. (*Picking up the packed box.*)

ROSENBERG. He did well managing the Reagans' finances, but, Chris, your affairs are very …

CHRISTOPHER. (*Crossing to him with box in hand.*) Mr. Rosenberg, you have to go back. (*HE crosses left, up around sofa to up center.*)

ROSENBERG. So, you've got your finances straightened out, but what about your romantic life?

CHRISTOPHER. What about it? (*Puts box underneath sofa table.*)

ROSENBERG. (*Crossing up to him.*) You've got Walter on hold. You don't know if you love him or hate him. This has nothing to do with me, but your life is still in complete upheaval.

CHRISTOPHER. (*Packing another box on sofa table.*) I don't know what to do about Walter. I want him in my life, but I'm afraid. Everyone I love dies. I'm a jinx.

ROSENBERG. On the basis of that lunatic statement alone, I'd say you need me at least until retirement age.

(*The INTERCOM buzzes. CHRIS crosses to answer it.*)

CHRISTOPHER. (*Into intercom.*) Who is it?

WALTER. (*On intercom.*) It's me, Walter.

ROSENBERG. Buzz him in.

CHRISTOPHER. (*Does so.*) I can't believe Walter would make the first move. Hey, you did some sort of weird poltergeist thing, didn't you?

ROSENBERG. (*Crossing up to him.*) Alright, I put the idea in Walter's noggin that you'd phoned him and asked him over. Don't ask me how. It's like the riddle of the sphinx.

(The DOORBELL rings. CHRIS answers it. WALTER is sheepishly in the doorway.)

CHRISTOPHER. Hi.

WALTER. Hi.

CHRISTOPHER. *(Gestures inside.)* Please.

WALTER. Sure.

CHRISTOPHER. Sit.

WALTER. Thanks. *(HE crosses to sofa and sits.)*

CHRISTOPHER. Water?

WALTER. No.

ROSENBERG. Would one of you say a sentence with a noun and a verb?

CHRISTOPHER. *(Sitting sofa arm left.)* Walter, I've been thinking a lot about us.

ROSENBERG. That's a little better, but get mushy. Go for broke. Forget my sensitivities.

CHRISTOPHER. *(Annoyed with Rosenberg.)* I am trying.

WALTER. What are you trying to say?

CHRISTOPHER. I'm trying to say that ... we're both such complicated people that it's inevitable that something would go wrong. But, maybe if we made a little effort. I mean, you could try to be less obnoxious.

ROSENBERG. This is the way to patch things up?

CHRISTOPHER. Okay, not obnoxious. Irritating. If not irritating, annoying.

ROSENBERG. I'm jumping in. *(HE crosses left to directly behind Christopher.)*

CHRISTOPHER. Don't you come near me.

WALTER. I won't. (*Getting up and around sofa arm right.*) Look, I'm tired of being Rhoda Reject.

ROSENBERG. I'm sorry. I've got to. Hold on, kiddo.

(*ROSENBERG grabs Christopher by the shoulders from behind. CHRIS moans. The LIGHTS change. CHRIS is now channeling Rosenberg. ROSENBERG speaks and CHRIS is forced to mouth the words like a ventriloquist's dummy.*)

WALTER. Chris, are you alright?

ROSENBERG. (*Through Chris.*) Walter Zuckerman, you plunge me into an emotional maelstrom. You are the most wonderful person. The greatest lover I've ever had. The technique, the passion, the stamina. Why you … you Hebraic sex machine. It's an absurdity for us to break up. Walter, there is an old saying, "*Es vet zich oys-hailen fur de chasseneh.*" Loose translation, "Everything heals in time for the wedding." Catch my drift, kiddo?

(*ROSENBERG lets go of Chris with such force that CHRIS sails into Walter's lap.*)

ROSENBERG. Oy, I've got to stop.

WALTER. Are you okay?

CHRISTOPHER. (*Composing himself.*) I think so.

WALTER. Chris, I don't know what you're trying to say.

CHRISTOPHER. (*Taking Walter by the arms.*) Walter, this is me now. (*Kneeling next to him and speaking quietly.*) I love you. I've always loved you. I do love you.

WALTER. (*Emotionally.*) Really? (*HE kneels next to Chris, embracing him.*) You really do? Oh, God.

ROSENBERG. (*Exhausted.*) I feel like I've run a marathon in an open toe pump.

WALTER. We really have to try to be more open with each other.

CHRISTOPHER. (*Sitting back on sofa, still holding onto Walter.*) I will. I will try.

WALTER. (*Joining him.*) You can tell me anything. You know I'm never judgmental.

ROSENBERG. He's a very open minded individual.

CHRISTOPHER. There is something I've always wanted to tell you. A secret I've kept for a long time.

WALTER. You do have two kidneys, don't you?

CHRISTOPHER. Yes. I have two kidneys and a ghost named Seymour Rosenberg.

WALTER. Huh?

ROSENBERG. (*Sitting on sofa arm left.*) Not a good move, son.

CHRISTOPHER. Mr. Rosenberg is here in the room with us. I can see him, but nobody else can. We talk, we laugh, we watch TV.

WALTER. I don't believe this.

CHRISTOPHER. Why do you think I ordered the Playboy channel?

WALTER. This isn't a joke, is it?

CHRISTOPHER. No joke. He's always looking over my shoulder like a Yiddishe Jiminy Cricket.

WALTER. Chris, just now you told me you loved me. That was a very critical emotional breakthrough for you. Now is when you should really start intensive psychotherapy. You can afford it now. But outside of the therapist's office, please don't tell anyone about this ghost thing.

ROSENBERG. (*Crossing down and sitting in the barber chair.*) It's just you and me, kid.

(*We hear COMMOTION in the hall. The door bursts open. POLLY enters, followed by WANDA WANG and LENORE. POLLY sees Walter and embraces him.*)

POLLY. Walter, darling! Have you two reconciled? I desperately need to believe in romance.

ROSENBERG. The Andrews Sisters from hell.

CHRISTOPHER. What are all of you doing together?

POLLY. Lunch, darling. It's extremely stimulating when three powerful women break bread.

WANDA. My idea. I have several projects on my plate. You know, your sister has a keen executive eye.

LENORE. And I have strong creative urges. (*Crossing down to Chris.*) Chris, I have, shall we say, come to smoke the peace pipe. For the past week, I have done a great deal of soul searching. I have walked through the fire and emerged cleansed.

CHRISTOPHER. You don't hate me?

LENORE. Hate is not a word in my vocabulary. For days after the broadcast, I lay in bed, drank very few fluids, ate nothing save for an occasional Jenny Craig entree. I have starved myself into a new awareness. It wasn't easy having the press dub me, "The Princess of Greed."

WALTER. I was amazed at all the coverage you and Chris got after the show.

LENORE. Those awful Paparazzi photos.

CHRISTOPHER. You're famous.

LENORE. I am famous. I'll tell you when it hit me. Leonard and I were in a cab in the Village and I guess we were around Seventh Avenue and we saw four, count 'em four drag queens dressed ... as *me*!

WANDA. (*Crossing down left between Lenore and Chris.*) Look, I don't have all day. I'm receiving an honorary doctorate at four. (*To Chris.*) I want you and Lenore to be on my show next Thursday. "Enemies Who Bond."

CHRISTOPHER. I'm not sure we have.

LENORE. Be gracious. My image needs work.

POLLY. And there's more.

CHRISTOPHER. More?

WANDA. My staff can't even handle all the mail we received after your show. I tip my hat. You stole it right out from under me. I want to create a show around you.

WALTER. What kind of show?

WANDA. It's called "Can You Believe This?" We send Chris all over the country to rout out the weirdest, freakiest nuts ever to parade in front of a camera.

CHRISTOPHER. This is too much.

WANDA. I've got files of 'em. Witches in Milwaukee. Cannibals in Terre Haute. Chrissy, isn't it a pisser?

WALTER. I don't know. I don't think Chris should carry the whole show. He should be the comic relief. Essentially, he's a humorist.

ROSENBERG. You're fortunate to have him. A good Jewish wife.

POLLY. I totally agree with Walter. Chris needs someone to play off of. Someone with a very dynamic personality and stage experience.

ROSENBERG. Her you need to watch out for.

(POLLY crosses around sofa table to join WANDA, LENORE and WALTER left.)

ROSENBERG. I think the show would be better if you ...

(The whole room becomes a strategy session for Chris' new show, as EVERYONE puts in their two cents, except for CHRIS, who seems to have been inadvertently left out. HE crosses down right.)

CHRISTOPHER. Excuse me. (*No one responds.*) Excuse me! (*Silence.*) I don't see a co-host at all. I also don't think the show should be limited to just the grotesque. The fun would be to see me, with my particular outlook, infiltrating the Ku Klux Klan, or Saddam Hussein's headquarters, or the Palm Springs home of Bob and Delores Hope.

ROSENBERG. (*Crossing down to Chris' left.*) I don't see you and Hope. Tell them we'll take a meeting next week.

CHRISTOPHER. Mr. Rosenberg, this is my show.

ROSENBERG. Be careful. You're blowing my cover.

CHRISTOPHER. I don't care. Call me Barbra Streisand, but I need control.

LENORE. Back up a minute. (*Slowly rising.*) Were you just conversing with my late father?

WALTER. (*Leaning in to Wanda.*) He's just slightly unhinged, not enough to jeopardize any deal.

POLLY. He's an original.

LENORE. (*Crossing slowly to just left of Rosenberg, opposite Chris.*) You were talking to my father. He's in this room, isn't he?

ROSENBERG. Put a lid on this quickly.

CHRISTOPHER. No, it's time you were outed.

WANDA. I see a classic *Wanda*.

CHRISTOPHER. Mr. Rosenberg is here.

(*The WHOLE ROOM gasps.*)

WANDA. Like an energy field?

CHRISTOPHER. Like an agent.

ROSENBERG. I am deeply offended.

LENORE. I sensed it all along. I have done a great deal of research into the occult sciences. Oh, yes. People have scoffed. (*SHE raises her hands, to "feel" Rosenberg's vibration and begins crossing left, up and around sofa to up center.*) Daddy? Daddy?

WANDA. Chris, does Mr. Rosenberg visit you often?

CHRISTOPHER. Generally speaking, it's easier finding Mr. Rosenberg than the super in this building.

ROSENBERG. I am not moving.

LENORE. We need to make our peace. I need closure.

ROSENBERG. It's all about her. I'll be damned if I give her any peace of mind. (*Crossing away up right.*)

(*LENORE continues her search. SHE continues crossing right, up and off through the archway. Fascinated, WANDA follows, watching her go off and sitting at the stool just below archway opening. ROSENBERG also watches, in amazement.*)

WALTER. Chris, this whole thing is a warped fantasy of yours. Your desperate need for a father.

CHRISTOPHER. Not so desperate.

POLLY. It's not a fantasy. If anyone could see a ghost, it would be Chris. (*Disgusted, WALTER retires to the Giacometti chair down left.*) When we were kids, you swore you saw Mother's spirit hovering over the skunk cabbage. If Mr. Rosenberg is indeed in this room, then I want to see him. I'm an artist. I have imagination. Why shouldn't I see him?

CHRISTOPHER. (*Crossing center to her.*) Because he's my ghost. Whatever I have, you want.

LENORE. (*Offstage.*) Daddy, release the poisons.

POLLY. (*Seductively taking off jacket.*) Mr. Rosenberg, I can see why you'd prefer not to speak to Lenore, but you and I have always been simpatico,

(*Crossing left and up center to cigarette box on sofa table.*) be a darling and light my cigarette.

ROSENBERG. You tell your sister that I will not be performing any parlor tricks for her amusement.

POLLY. Mr. R., have you ever snuck into my room while I was nude? I've always felt like I was being watched.

ROSENBERG. Not once. Not ever.

POLLY. (*Crossing right, down around sofa, sitting sofa center.*) Wait 'til you see what I've got in store for you tonight.

LENORE. You are speaking to my father. (*Suddenly struck with an idea, SHE rushes down to left of coffee table, takes off a ring and kneels.*) Daddy, take my marcasite ring and make it spin like a dredel.

WANDA. (*Up and crossing down, right of sofa, setting the imaginary camera angle.*) Push in for a close-up.

POLLY. Oh, I feel him on me. Oh, his touch is so ... Oh, God.

(*LENORE, repulsed, crosses up left.*)

ROSENBERG. Get her to knock it off.

CHRISTOPHER. (*Taunting Rosenberg.*) Mr. Rosenberg, get off my sister. You should be ashamed of yourself. He's old enough to be her grandfather.

ROSENBERG. You're as bad as she is.

POLLY. (*Writhing on the sofa.*) I can't take it. This powerful, coarsing feeling. Overwhelming, cataclysmic.

LENORE. (*Cheating down a step, then back.*) I pray my dead mother can't hear this.

WALTER. This isn't happening.

ROSENBERG. I've never been so humiliated.

POLLY. Dear God, he's entered me!

LENORE. (*Rushing to up left sofa.*) Daddy!!!

(*This is the final straw for ROSENBERG, who lifts a large vase of roses and hurls its contents at Polly. WALTER screams.*)

WALTER. (*Running up to left of sofa.*) There is a ghost! The dead walk among us!

CHRISTOPHER. (*Crossing to survey the damage.*) And my sofa's drenched. (*HE starts to swoon.*) Ohhh. (*His body is undergoing a change. HE almost falls.*)

WALTER. (*Seeing Chris in trouble, HE runs down and helps Chris to the coffee table.*) Chris, are you alright?

(*The LIGHTS change. CHRISTOPHER is channeling another entity. HE begins speaking in the voice of Rosenberg's dead wife, MIRIAM, which sounds remarkably like Lenore.*)

CHRISTOPHER. (*As Miriam.*) Why am I moving so quickly? It's turbulent. What am I doing in this garishly over-decorated parlor?

ROSENBERG. (*Crossing slowly down right.*) Miriam!

LENORE. (*Crossing slowly down left and sitting in the Giacometti chair.*) It's my mother. My mother's voice is emanating from Chris' physicality.

WANDA. He's channeling. We've done six shows on this.

LENORE. Mother, it's Lenore. Are you happy?

CHRISTOPHER. (*As Miriam.*) *Comme ci, comme ça.* It's not all cappuccinos and screenings of *Les Enfants du Paradis*, but it's peaceful. Sy, it's not like you to be so quiet. Are you angry with me about something?

ROSENBERG. No, Miriam, I'm not angry with you. But, me, my terrible failings.

CHRISTOPHER. (*As Miriam.*) You've been talking to Sheldon. Sy, your brother's a kook.

ROSENBERG. He heard everything. That awful day in the hospital. He heard you vilify me. I'll never forget it. It was like a brand.

CHRISTOPHER. (*As Miriam.*) You listen to me, Sy. I was in excruciating pain. If I recall correctly, I died shortly afterwards. Some allowances, please. Yes, I'm sure I said ugly, violent things, but ...

ROSENBERG. And I deserved them. I treated you as an acquisition, not as a partner. I was always playing a role, the father, the great provider, the loving husband. It was all a sham.

CHRISTOPHER. (*As Miriam.*) There is a grain of truth in that. Oh, yes. But, darling, there was so much more. Don't let Sheldon or any other of your *schnorring* relatives take that away from us. Remember the summers at Saranac Lake? The trip to Japan? Lenore, all of seven, taking over the tea ceremony. Believe me, the good was plentiful, bountiful. Now, enough of this foolishness, come back to me.

ROSENBERG. I will soon, but I have things I need to do here.

CHRISTOPHER. (*As Miriam.*) Sy, you were needed and you've done good. The young man is on his way. Now, leave it be.

ROSENBERG. I can't. I went away too soon. It's not just for him. I want to be here. It's not fair. I need a little more time.

CHRISTOPHER. (*As Miriam.*) Darling, there is no more time. You know it's not right to linger. If you truly love the young man, you will let him go. Let the living live.

ROSENBERG. (*Moved.*) Let the living live. (*Smiling.*) You always knew how to turn a phrase.

CHRISTOPHER. (*As Miriam.*) Now, turn left and go out that door. It's remarkably simple.

ROSENBERG. I'll be with you shortly. (*To himself.*) Let the living live.

CHRISTOPHER. (*As Miriam.*) Oh, my, this crossing of the borders of the beyond is extremely taxing. *A bientôt,* dear.

ROSENBERG. Good-bye, Miriam, my love.

(*The SPIRIT starts to leave.*)

LENORE. Wait a minute. Mother, don't you have anything to say to me?

CHRISTOPHER. (*As Miriam.*) Lenore, you're way too thin. It's aging. Otherwise, my precious baby, I am so proud of you. Grace in defeat. Now that shows character.

(*The LIGHTS change. CHRIS is suddenly hurled out of the trance onto the floor down center. POLLY and WALTER rush to help him up. WALTER left and POLLY right of him.*)

POLLY. Chris?
CHRISTOPHER. Quite a sensation.
WALTER. You're amazing.
WANDA. What a talent!
ROSENBERG. What a kid. What a man. I guess this is goodbye.
CHRISTOPHER. (*Crossing to Rosenberg.*) Mr. Rosenberg, you know I never meant to hurt you. But this is the way it has to be.
ROSENBERG. You going to be okay?
CHRISTOPHER. It's funny, I suppose I've been surrounding myself with ghosts all my life. This will be the first time I'm really alone. (*Noticing Walter, HE backs up slightly and takes Walter's hand.*) Although, I won't really be alone.
ROSENBERG. I feel like I'm in one of those prison pictures you like so much. Sy Rosenberg walking the last mile. Let's get it over with. (*HE crosses to the doorway, followed by CHRIS.*)

(WALTER, POLLY and WANDA, totally in awe of the situation, follow en masse, to the doorway. At the door, CHRISTOPHER nods to Rosenberg to make some sort of gesture to Lenore. ROSENBERG balks but CHRIS is firm. ROSENBERG agrees. ROSENBERG picks a single rose up from the floor, crosses down left, and tenderly hands it to Lenore. EVERYONE is rapt. LENORE closes her eyes and accepts it. SHE and her father have made their peace. MR. ROSENBERG returns to the doorway and looks at Christopher one last time.)

ROSENBERG. Shalom, kiddo. *(HE throws open the door and exits.)*

(We hear the same other worldly SOUND EFFECT as when Rosenberg first arrived, followed by the faint tinkling of BELLS. CHRIS closes the door.)

LENORE. He's gone.
POLLY. *(Crossing up to the door and hugging Chris.)* Chris, that was incredible. Think of all the fabulous dead people we can invite to parties!
CHRISTOPHER. *(Transfixed.)* I've got an idea.
WANDA. For the show?
CHRISTOPHER. I know exactly what I must do with my ten million dollars. I don't need a new house. I'm going to need every bit of cash to build the Seymour L. Rosenberg Center for Jewish Studies!
POLLY. Have you gone mad?

CHRISTOPHER. (*Crossing to Lenore.*) Lenore, your father must never be forgotten.

POLLY. But, all of your money?

CHRISTOPHER. Marble's expensive.

WALTER. He's flipping out.

CHRISTOPHER. It's simple. Mr. Rosenberg gave me his money and I'm giving it back to his people.

LENORE. I'm his people!

WALTER. Chris, please don't think I'm trying to take over, but you need psychiatric help. Just a little counseling.

POLLY. (*Following Walter's path.*) Christopher, I know how you feel. I think it's marvelous. If you would like to convert, I will convert with you. In fact, we'll make a day of it. However, giving all of your money ...

CHRISTOPHER. Polly, I've made up my mind. I'm a different person now.

(The INTERCOM buzzes. CHRIS crosses to answer it.)

POLLY. (*Dejectedly falling onto the sofa.*) Well, you don't expect me to give all my John Galianos back.

CHRISTOPHER. (*Into intercom.*) Who is it?

MALE VOICE. (*On Intercom.*) Federal Express for Ladendorf.

CHRISTOPHER. (*Into intercom.*) We're on the second floor. (*Buzzing him in.*)

WALTER. (*Crossing up to Chris at door.*) Chris, join me in couple's therapy.

(CHRIS opens the door, steps out into the hall and waits for his package.)

POLLY. Family therapy. I'll join you.
LENORE. Group therapy. I'll join you. Another hour a week can't hurt.

(CHRISTOPHER returns with an envelope and closes the door.)

WALTER. What is it?
CHRISTOPHER. *(Crossing right and then down to barber chair.)* It's from an attorney's office. Miller, Miller, Goff and Gold. *(HE scans the contents of the envelope, then sits in the chair.)* It's about Norma Leeds.
POLLY. The old witch who died across the hall? I need a drink. *(SHE gets up, crosses left and up around sofa to liquor up center. Filling her glass, SHE crosses around and down right to just above the barber chair.)*
CHRISTOPHER. *(Reading.)* "Though Mrs. Leeds may have appeared destitute, she was on the contrary, an extremely wealthy, if eccentric, woman. To reward you for your years of kindness and generosity to your neighbor, Mrs. Leeds has bequeathed to you the bulk of her estate to the sum of fifteen million dollars. Sincerely, Louis R. Miller. Be prepared for her nephew to contest."
LENORE. *(Rising.)* Whatever you're doing, keep it up.
POLLY. *(Wearily.)* So, who are we giving this money to? The Evelyn Wood School of Speed Reading?

CHRISTOPHER. We're giving none of this away. (*Crossing to center of sofa.*) For one thing, we've got to move out of this dump. Wanda, it's a good thing you're here. Saves me the dime.

WANDA. I'm here for you, bud.

CHRISTOPHER. Kids, we've got another lawsuit on our hands. We're going back on TV. (*HE reaches right, pulling Walter over sofa arm right and sits.*) Walter, I'm going to need your help.

(*LENORE joins them and sits sofa right. WANDA sits sofa left and POLLY perches on the up stage right sofa corner. The FIVE of them enthusiastically plot their new strategy as the CURTAIN falls.*)

CURTAIN

ALTERNATE SCENES

In our production economics forced us to have one female understudy cover all three of the women's roles. To allow for greater versatility, we cast a Caucasian actress. When she went on as Wanda Wang, we performed an alternate version. I'm offering it here in case you are in the same situation or unfortunately are unable to find an Asian actress to play Wanda Wang. Whenever the name Wanda Wang was mentioned, we changed it to Wanda Wilson. The name of the TV show on her set was simply WANDA.

(*WANDA enters ...*)

POLLY. Hello.
WANDA. Hello. Wanda Wilson.
POLLY. I'm Polly Lawrence and this is my brother, Christopher Ladendorf and this is Chris' publicist, Walter Zuckerman.

Page 85

WANDA. (*To Chris.*) No, I don't. I understand what you're saying very well. (*To camera.*) I was a fat, little, Lithuanian girl from Milwaukee. But I had a teacher. An English teacher in the eighth grade, Mrs. Laspina. She was the only person who would give that chubby little kid any encouragement. It certainly wasn't my mother. But that's another show. Anything Wanda Wilson has achieved is due to Mrs. Laspina.

All other mentions of Oakland should be changed to Milwaukee.

COSTUME PLOT

ACT I
Scene 1

<u>Mr. Rosenberg</u>: (1) dark suit, white shirt, tie with matching pocket square, black dress shoes. (2) short kimono over boxer shorts, socks with garters, same shoes

<u>Christopher</u>: black jeans, Mandarin collar shirt, slip-on sandals, adds white lab coat onstage

<u>Polly</u>: dark dress over slip, necklace, earrings, high heels; carrying decorated leather jacket, boa

Scene 2

<u>Polly</u>: long, elegant evening gown with necklace; adds matching high heels, elbow-length gloves, net shawl, earrings, evening bag onstage

<u>Christopher</u>: (1) India print robe over tank top, drawstring pants, sandals (I-1); (2) black tuxedo with white shirt, black tie, black dress pumps

<u>Mr. Rosenberg</u>: second dark suit, striped shirt, second tie with matching pocket square, shoes (I-1)

Scene 3

<u>Polly</u>: robe, slippers

<u>Mr. Rosenberg</u>: sport shirt, trousers (I-2), shoes (I-1); add kimono (I-1)

<u>Christopher</u>: T-shirt, pants (I-2), sandals (I-1), add lab coat (I-1) onstage

<u>Walter</u>: dark slacks, light long-sleeved sport shirt, dark loafers

Scene 4

Polly: dark short pleated skirt, camisole, starched short-sleeved white blouse, tie, high-heeled Mary Jane shoes

Walter: slacks (I-3), long-sleeved button-down shirt, tie, loafers (I-3)

Christopher: light slacks, matching vest, button-down shirt, striped tie, Madras jacket, saddle shoes

Lenore: dress, high heels, lots of gold jewelry, purse

Mr. Rosenberg: third suit, white shirt, third tie with matching pocket square, shoes (I-1)

ACT II
Scene 1

Christopher: jeans (I-1), Hawaiian shirt, high-top sneakers

Mr. Rosenberg: repeat (I-4)

Polly: dark, sleeveless dress, necklace, bracelet, earrings, large-brimmed hat, sunglasses, shoes (I-1)

Walter: Long-sleeved silk shirt, dark suit pants, dark dress shoes

Scene 2

Walter: Repeat II-1 with suit jacket and tie

Polly: Chanel-type jacket over sheath, Chanel-type purse, high heels

Christopher: sports jacket, button-down shirt, light slacks, loafers

Wanda Wang: tailored business suit, high heels, jewelry

<u>Lenore:</u> Ultrasuede suit, flowered blouse, lots of jewelry, high heels

<u>Mr. Rosenberg:</u> repeat I-4

Scene 3

<u>Christopher:</u> silk pajamas, Chinese robe, sandals (I-1)

<u>Mr. Rosenberg:</u> repeat I-4

<u>Walter:</u> sports shirt, light slacks, shoes (I-3)

<u>Polly:</u> flowered dress with matching jacket, high heels, purse (II-2)

<u>Lenore:</u> jumpsuit, long openwork sweater, high heels, large purse

<u>Wanda Wang:</u> second tailored suit, scarf, purse, shoes (II-2)

PROPERTY PLOT

FURNITURE:

Large sofa with eight pillows, two throws
Coffee table
Reclining barber chair
Desk with desk chair
Sofa table (long, high table upstage of sofa)
Flimsy three-legged stool ("Giacometti chair")
Upholstered stool

ACT I
Scene 1
Tray with 2 teacups, 2 saucers, filled teapot, spoon, sugar
   packet, cream packet
Ice pack
Wallet with money
Framed wedding photo
Tray with 4 medals
Pitch pipe
Human hair diagram (on roller shade, preferably)
Shelf with 8 decorated yams
Envelope with 4 photos
Appointment book
2 suitcases
Hatbox
Dead amaryllis plant
1 pair disposable plastic gloves
Gooseneck lamp with detachable shade

Wall-mounted paper towel roll
Container with cotton balls
Alcohol bottle
Electrolysis goggles
Electrolysis machine with foot pedal and pen attachment

Scene 2
Rabbit's foot
2 condom packages
Wire coat hanger
Desk lamp
Sofa table lamp

Scene 3
Telephone
Second pair disposable plastic gloves
Air conditioner in window
    As in Scene 1:
    Gooseneck lamp with detachable shade
    Wall-mounted paper towel roll
    Container with cotton balls
    Alcohol bottle
    Electrolysis goggles
    Electrolysis machine with foot pedal and pen attachment
    Flimsy three-legged stool ("Giacometti chair")

Scene 4
Feather duster
Wall-mounted folding ironing board
Iron

Extension cord
Plate with crackers and cheese
Briefcase with pen, document and cellular phone

ACT II
Scene 1
House keys
Laundry basket with two folded shirts, other clothing,
    detergent
Black fabric
Pin cushion with pins
4 shopping bags

Scene 2
"Talk Show" panels
3 chairs
Clipboard with itinerary

Scene 3
2 packing boxes
Several piles of books
Cigarette box with cigarettes
Vase with roses
Federal Express envelope with letter

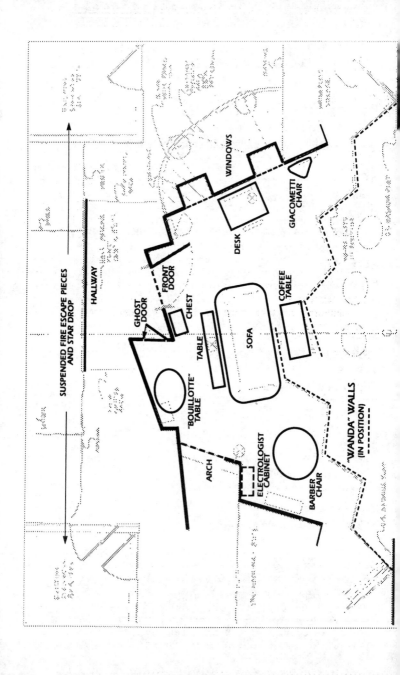

SUSPENDED FIRE ESCAPE PIECES AND STAR DROP

HALLWAY

WINDOWS

DESK

GIACOMETTI CHAIR

FRONT DOOR

GHOST DOOR

CHEST

TABLE

SOFA

COFFEE TABLE

"BOUILLOTTE" TABLE

ARCH

ELECTROLOGIST CABINET

BARBER CHAIR

"WANDA" WALLS
(IN POSITION)

WHAT THE BELLHOP SAW
(Little Theatre)
(FARCE)

by Wm. Van Zandt and Jane Milmore

8 male, 4 female

The play starts with a rather nice fellow checking into a $400.00 suite in "New York City's finest hotel". From there it snowballs into a fabulous nightmare involving a Salman Rushdie-type author, an Iranian Terrorist, a monstrous shrew-like woman, a conniving bellboy, a monumentally incompetent F.B.I. man, a nubile celebrity-mad maid, a dim-witted secretary, and a cute little pigtailed girl. All the while, gag lines are popping at Orville Redenbacher speed. Everything happens at pretty much whirlwind velocity. This latest farce by Van Zandt and Milmore combines topical humor with the traditional antics of farce: doors slamming, characters careening and confusion reigning supreme. A wildly funny farce! An excellent piece of workmanship by our two authors who take pride in the old-fashioned craft of comedy writing. #25062

THE SENATOR WORE PANTYHOSE
(Little Theatre)
(COMEDY)

by Wm. Van Zandt and Jane Milmore

7 male, 3 female

If you're tired of political and religious scandals, this is your greatest revenge! Van Zandt & Milmore's latest comedy revolves around the failing Presidential campaign of "Honest" Gabby Sandalson, a regular guy whose integrity has all but crippled his bid for the White House. Desparate for votes, his sleazeball campaign manager trumps up an implausible sex scandal which accidentally backfires on PMS Club leader Reverend Johnny and his makeup-faced wife Honey Pie; an opportunistic innkeeper with a penchant for antique food; the town's wayward single girl; two escaped convicts looking for stolen loot; and newscaster Don Bother. "A guaranteed hit!" (Asbury Park Press) "The characters swap beds, identities and jabs in what may be a flawless sex farce." (The Register). #21084

ROAD TO NIRVANA
by Arthur Kopit

Dark comedy
Advanced Groups

(2m., 2f. 2 exts.)Ex-movie mogul Al has invited his old pal Jerry, another ex-mogul, over for a visit, to do lunch, take a meeting, and so on. Jerry is pretty desperate to get back into the film business. He has been producing educational films the past few years, ever since Al fired him, after first screwing his wife, who then committed suicide. In other words, Jerry's life and career is basically in the toilet; still he comes to Al's house, enticed by a vague promise of re-entry into the intoxicating world of Hollywood deal-making. Al is also on the skids; but he has a hot property, and needs Jerry to co-produce it with him. It seems the world's hottest female rock star has written an autobiographical screenplay and is willing to star in it herself—if, that is, she can find a producer willing to meet her terms. Apparently, Al has already met these terms. He has slit his wrists to demonstrate his commitment to the project, and he wants Jerry to do the same. Jerry is, of course, very reluctant—particularly when he learns that the "screenplay" is, word-for-word, *Moby Dick*—except that Nirvana, the rock star, has substituted herself for Ahab and a huge penis for the great white whale! Ridiculous, you say? Of course—but that's Hollywood, the living, breathing, real-life theatre of the absurd. Jerry finally does cut his wrists, and undergoes other degrading acts to demonstrate his wish to be a part of the Big Deal. In the second act, we meet the whacked-out Nirvana—and we learn just what it is that Al needs Jerry to consummate the deal. Jerry is asked to prove his commitment *again:* Nirvana wants his balls. She already has Al's; but she wants more. And Jerry must *really, finally* decide just how much he wants to make the deal. "Mr. Kopit arouses audiences with his acerbity, his pitch-black humor and his sheer virulence."—N.Y. Times. "Careens madly from farce to fantasy and back again, and it makes for a consistently entertaining evening."—Louisville Courier-Journal. "A malicious and effective send-up of David Mamet's *Speed-the-Plow*, yet it has a vigor, and a vinegar, of its own."—Time Mag. "Gruffly announcing itself as scurrilous talk, it rapidly escalates into a dirty joke—funny enough to make you hoarse,.then into an outsize legend before, finally, rounding itself off as the equivalent of a modern morality play."—Boston Globe.   (#20134)

Other Publications for Your Interest

THE ROCKY HORROR SHOW
(MUSICAL)
Book, music and lyrics by RICHARD O'BRIEN

7 men, 3 women. Various ints. and exts.

At last! The original stage version of the cult movie that has been a "12 O'clock high" for thousands of enthusiastic movie-goers. Live, on stage, see Dr. Frank N. Furter match wits (?) with the innocent young newlyweds! Thrill to the delightfully trashy rock and roll music! "It isn't a play, it isn't a musical, it isn't a rock concert... It's a sort of glitter, rock, horror, comedy, tranvestite circus... And if you love—say, 'Sound of Music'—you will probably hate it."—WABC-TV. "*The Rocky Horror Show* is a sicko-wacko-weirdo rock concert. It keeps trying to blow your mind with loud music and perverted sexuality, but it is so simple-minded, and so completely silly, that it ends up being a lot of fun. It may get a cult following, even though there is no nudity."—NBC.

(#20049)

(Restricted. When available, Terms quoted on application—Music available on rental.) Posters Available

VAMPIRE LESBIANS OF SODOM
(ADVENTUROUS GROUPS.) FARCE
By CHARLES BUSCH

6 men, 2 women. Unit set

This truly bizarre entertainment, cut right out of the *Rocky Horror* genre, is about vamps, has nothing to do with lesbians and takes the audience from ancient Sodom to the Hollywood of the twenties, ending up somehow in present day Las Vegas. "Costumes flashier than pinball machines, outrageous lines, awful puns, sinister innocence, harmless depravity—it's all here. One can imagine a cult forming."—NY Times. "Bizarre and wonderful... If you think Boy George is a gender-bender, well, like Jolson said, you ain't seen nothing yet! Forget your genders, come on, get happy."—Broadway Mag. Published with *Sleeping Beauty*, or *Coma*. (Royalty, $50-$40.)

(#24006)

Other Publications for Your Interest

CINDERELLA WALTZ
(ALL GROUPS—COMEDY)
By DON NIGRO

4 men, 5 women—1 set

Rosey Snow is trapped in a fairy tale world that is by turns funny and a little frightening, with her stepsisters Goneril and Regan, her demented stepmother, her lecherous father, a bewildered Prince, a fairy godmother who sings salty old sailor songs, a troll and a possibly homicidal village idiot. A play which investigates the archetypal origins of the world's most popular fairy tale and the tension between the more familiar and charming Perrault version and the darker, more ancient and disturbing tale recorded by the brothers Grimm. Grotesque farce and romantic fantasy blend in a fairy tale for adults.

(#5208)

ROBIN HOOD
(LITTLE THEATRE—COMEDY)
By DON NIGRO

14 men, 8 women—(more if desired.) Unit set.

In a land where the rich get richer, the poor are starving, and Prince John wants to cut down Sherwood Forest to put up an arms manufactory, a slaughterhouse and a tennis court for the well to do, this bawdy epic unites elements of wild farce and ancient popular mythologies with an environmentalist assault on the arrogance of wealth and power in the face of poverty and hunger. Amid feeble and insane jesters, a demonic snake oil salesman, a corrupt and lascivious court, a singer of eerie ballads, a gluttonous lusty friar and a world of vivid and grotesque characters out of a Brueghel painting, Maid Marian loses her clothes and her illusions among the poor and Robin tries to avoid murder and elude the Dark Monk of the Wood who is Death and also perhaps something more.

(#20075)